2/15

HACKNEY LIBRARY SE

D0230365

THIS BOOK MUST BE RETURNED TO
BEFORE THE LAST DATE STAMPED. FINES MAY BE
CHARGED IF IT IS LATE. AVOID FINES BY RENEWING THE
BOOK.
(SUBJECT TO IT NOT BEING RESERVED).

PEOPLE WHO ARE OVER 60, UNDER 17 OR REGISTERED
DISABLED ARE NOT CHARGED FINES.   PS.6578

LONDON BOROUGH OF HACKNEY
3 8040 01497 1552

BE MY HERO

Nathalie Mayer is thirty-four. On the surface she's an attractive single woman running a successful bridal business. Despite her obvious delight in other people's weddings Nathalie has always declared a settled relationship is not for her. There has only ever been one man whom she felt she could love.

Evan Davies is back in town after a six year absence. Last time he was home, he and Nathalie had tentatively begun to take their friendship to a new level. Now he's back and has the reason for his sudden departure from six years ago with him – his daughter, Polly.

BE MY HERO

Be My Hero

by

Nell Dixon

Magna Large Print Books
Long Preston, North Yorkshire,
BD23 4ND, England.

British Library Cataloguing in Publication Data.

Dixon, Nell
    Be my hero.

    A catalogue record of this book is
    available from the British Library

    ISBN   978-0-7505-3655-4

LONDON BOROUGH OF
HACKNEY
LIBRARY SERVICES

LOCAT.	
ACC. No.	13 /008
CLASS	

First published in 2007 by Moonlit Romance Publishing, USA

Copyright © 2007 Nell Dixon

Cover illustration © Ilona Wellmann by arrangement with
Arcangel Images

The moral right of the author has been asserted

Published in Large Print 2013 by arrangement with
Nell Dixon

All Rights reserved. No part of this publication may be
reproduced, stored in a retrieval system, or transmitted in any
form or by any means, electronic, mechanical, photocopying,
recording or otherwise without the prior permission of the
Copyright owner.

Magna Large Print is an imprint of Library Magna Books Ltd.

Printed and bound in Great Britain by
T.J. (International) Ltd., Cornwall, PL28 8RW

All characters and circumstances
are the invention of the author.
Any resemblance to actual people
or events is purely coincidental.

To the consultants and staff of
Birmingham Womens Hospital
and especially Mr Afnan.
God is good.

Chapter One

Nathalie hurried over to the window as fast as discretion allowed, certain her eyes had played a trick on her. All around her, her brother's wedding guests chattered and circulated on the dance floor.

Nathalie's attention focused on the large picture window of the ballroom and the glimpse of the man she thought she had seen outside on the terrace.

'Nathalie, are you all right, dear?' Her mother's concerned tone snapped her out of her reverie.

'I'm fine, I thought ... never mind. I'll just go and get a drink.' She picked up the front of her long, dark red velvet gown and headed towards the bar area. One of her brothers would be sure to know if the man she thought she'd seen in the garden was really here.

'Hey, little sister,' Jerome – her older brother – called to her from the bar. Nate, her twin stood next to him. Dressed in their dark formal wedding suits, the family resemblance appeared even more marked than usual. Both men were tall, with black hair and piercing blue eyes. Jerome had a more devil-may-care appearance, Nathalie thought. He had a reckless edge, even in a wedding suit.

'You look flustered,' Nate observed, looking at her warm cheeks.

'Dancing always makes me thirsty.' She accepted one of the pre-poured glasses of juice which stood with the flutes of champagne on large silver trays all along the bar.

'Thank you so much for arranging all this for us today, Tali. Jenni and I couldn't have organised the wedding without you.'

Nathalie smiled at her twin. 'It is my job and I've enjoyed every minute. Although, a little more notice would have been nice,' she assured him.

'Has Jerome told you he ran into Evan in town yesterday?' Nate asked.

Nathalie took a big gulp of her drink, pressing her fingers hard against the glass so her hand wouldn't betray the shakiness, which had just come over her.

'No, he didn't mention it.' She was pleased her voice sounded cool and controlled, even if she didn't feel it.

'I met him outside the bank. I invited him

to drop in to the party today if he had a chance.' Jerome had a teasing look in his eyes as he watched her to see how she had taken the information. All of her brothers knew how she used to feel about Evan.

'When was he last in town? It's been a few years,' Nate said, before placing his empty glass back down on the bar and allowing himself to be steered off to greet some more guests by his bride.

Six years, Nathalie thought to herself. All the time he'd been gone she'd only heard the barest snippets of information. She didn't even know if he had married or started a family in that time.

'Look who I just found outside!' Barnaby, Nathalie's youngest brother called from the doorway. The prickling of the hairs on the nape of her neck and an inner sixth sense warned her who she would see when she turned around.

'Hello, Nathalie.'

The sound of her name spoken by Evan's cool, gravelly voice sent little butterflies of excitement skittering around in her stomach. She struggled to take a breath. 'Evan,' she acknowledged.

She decided he hadn't changed much in the last six years. Except he had a man's frame now, broad-chested and broad-shouldered. Small lines crinkled at the corners of his bright blue eyes and his hair had been cropped in a new short style.

'Glad you could make it. Have a drink.' Jerome passed him a glass of champagne.

'I wouldn't have missed this for the world. Where is the groom?' Evan looked around the crowded room.

'His bride spirited him off.' Barnaby helped himself to a glass.

'We'll go hunt him down,' Jerome offered. He and Barnaby walked away towards the dance floor, leaving Nathalie alone with Evan.

'So, how have you been?'

Nathalie swallowed. 'Fine. Busy. You?'

'The same.'

She felt the heat creep into her cheeks. This was ridiculous. She was thirty-four, not thirteen. He'd been gone all this time and he could still make her blush like a teenager.

'I guess now Nate's married, you'll be next.' He took a sip of his drink.

'What gives you that idea?' His statement surprised her. There was no one serious in her life. She dated, yes, but there had only been one man she had ever given her heart to, and he stood in front of her now. Six years after he'd walked out of her life without any warning.

'You and Nate are twins – you always did everything together, and you're a beautiful woman, Nathalie. It seemed a natural assumption.' He shrugged.

'How about you?' Her eyes darted automatically to his ring finger. She wondered where he'd been and what he'd been doing whilst he'd been gone. There were a million questions she longed to ask.

'I'm single. I was married for a while.' His expression hardened and the sudden appearance of ice in his eyes sent a chill along her spine.

'Oh. So what brings you back into town?' She decided to turn the conversation to a safer subject. That way she could ignore the inconvenient feeling of sweet relief that had swept through her when he'd said he was single.

'I'm visiting family. I'm looking for a house to buy, as I intend to settle back here.'

'I see.' Nathalie dropped her gaze and took a sip of her drink. Her mind worked overtime at his news.

'Evan!' Her brothers returned with Nate and Jenni.

Nathalie took advantage of her clan's

return to slip away and recover her composure. Meeting Evan had thrown her into a state of total confusion. Just an hour ago, she would have sworn she was so over Evan. Now, after seeing him again, she wasn't so sure. Nathalie never liked to feel unsure about anything.

If he moved back into town, it was inevitable she'd bump into him again. They had the same friends, had always moved in the same circles. He had been friends with her brothers for years as they had all grown up. How would she cope with seeing him all the time?

Her mother, slim and chic in her pastel blue dress, beckoned to her from the other side of the dance floor. 'Have you seen Jenni?'

'She's in the bar with Nate. Evan Davies has just arrived.'

Her mother's blue eyes – so like Nathalie's own – surveyed her shrewdly. 'How wonderful. I'd heard he'd come back. Jenni will need to go upstairs and change soon. I wondered if you could go and help her.'

Nathalie wondered why all of her family, except her, seemed to know that Evan was back in town. Keeping her thoughts to herself, she pinned a smile on her face for her

16

mother's benefit. 'Of course, I hadn't realised the time. I'll go and see if she's ready.'

Her mother patted her hand, much the way she had used to when Nathalie had been a small child in need of reassurance. 'Thank you, darling.'

Evan made small talk with his old friends in the bar but all his attention was given to their sister. Six years ago, he had been at another wedding where Nathalie had been the bridesmaid and he had been best man. It had been the same day he'd received the bombshell letter; the same day he'd left town without saying goodbye. That had been the last time he'd seen her – until today.

He remembered the first time they'd met. He and Jerome had played hooky from school to go fishing; they had been sixteen. They'd sneaked back to Jerome's house to get some snacks and drinks when a tall, skinny schoolgirl with jet black pigtails and flashing blue eyes had caught them in the kitchen. It had been pure bad luck that Nathalie had come home early for a dental appointment. Both he and Jerome had been grounded for a month for that escapade.

Nathalie rejoined the circle and spoke to her twin's new bride. 'Mum said to see if you wanted to get changed yet.'

Jenni nodded. 'Give me a minute.' She headed back towards the dance floor. Nate and his brothers turned to speak to another guest, and Evan found himself face-to-face with Nathalie for the second time that day.

'Here we are again.' He wished he'd said something less prosaic.

'Yes.'

'Nate told me that you organised all of this.'

She seemed glad of the conversational opening. 'I own a bridal shop and one of the services we offer is wedding planning. Nate and Jenni only got engaged at Christmas, so a Valentine's day wedding was a little short notice, but if I couldn't help my own brother – well...' She shrugged.

Evan surveyed the faint flush along Nathalie's high cheekbones. 'You were a bridesmaid last time I saw you.'

Her expression changed, and for a moment, Evan saw the fourteen-year-old-girl from the kitchen all those years ago.

'Yes, well, thanks for reminding me of that!' She snapped. 'Excuse me, I have to help Jenni.'

He watched her go in search of Nate's bride, and cursed his own idiocy. Nathalie

18

hadn't needed to be reminded of the last time they'd met. Some things didn't alter – he'd made a mess of things then and he'd made a mess of them again now. It hadn't been very tactful to remind her of the way he'd treated her.

Absentmindedly, he took another sip of champagne and sighed as Nathalie continued to walk away through the crowd with Jenni and another bridesmaid.

Nathalie's hands shook as she attempted to unfasten the tiny seed pearl buttons on the back of Jenni's bridal gown.

'Here, let me.' Jenni's other bridesmaid offered to help.

'It's not like you to be all fingers and thumbs,' Jenni remarked as she craned her neck to see what her two helpers were doing.

'I'm sorry.' Nathalie picked up the clothes hanger, ready to help Jenni remove her dress for hanging.

'He did look very nice.' Jenni stepped out of the pool of white silk.

Nathalie's cheeks flamed. 'Who? Evan's just an old friend of Jerome's.'

Two pairs of eyes looked at her with interest.

'I used to have a crush on him. Then we

dated for a while before he left town a few years ago.' Nathalie bent to pick up Jenni's dress and hide her hot cheeks.

'Methinks the lady doth protest too much.' Jenni laughed.

Nathalie placed Jenni's dress on the padded hanger and zipped up the protective cover with care. 'We'd better hurry, the car will be here for you and Nate soon.'

'I'd better not keep my husband waiting. I have to toss my bouquet.' She smiled at Nathalie.

Nathalie ignored Jenni's comment about the bouquet. Her new sister-in-law meant well, but Nathalie had no wish to become a bride. Romance and fairy-tale weddings were for other people. She had resigned herself a long time ago to remaining the bridesmaid and never the bride. Hadn't Evan just reminded her of that?

Nate had waited on the staircase for his bride to reappear so they could say their farewells to the guests before setting off on honeymoon. Nathalie joined her parents at the foot of the stairs with the other guests as the final photographs were taken.

'I'm glad he's finally happy,' her mother murmured.

'Me too.' Nathalie felt pleased her twin

had managed to put his past behind him, but she couldn't help feeling sad, knowing the same kind of happiness wasn't destined to be hers.

'Okay, get ready!' Jenni called as she turned her back to the crowd and prepared to toss her bouquet.

It was pure, instinctive reflexes which brought Nathalie's hand up in time to catch the posy of scarlet roses and green ferns as it came winging towards her.

Her brothers whooped as she made a perfect catch and the guests standing around her congratulated her.

'Your turn next, dear.' Her father patted her arm and moved off with the rest of the family to see the bridal couple leave. Nathalie stood still for a moment and bent her head to inhale the deep, rich scent of the flowers in her hand. Ridiculous superstition!

'Are you coming to see them off?' Evan's voice, deep and masculine in her ear, made her jump. Deep in thought, she hadn't realised he was still there.

'Of course!' She drew a deep breath. 'I'm sorry, I didn't mean to snap.'

'No, it's okay. I think it's me who owes you the apology for earlier.'

Nathalie forced a smile, her nerves felt ragged and raw. 'Then we had better put it behind us.' She took a step forward ready to leave, only to still again as Evan slipped his arm through hers to escort her.

Her pulse thudded as he walked with her to where the wedding guests were sprinkling more confetti and tying the last tin can on to the back of Nate and Jenni's wedding car.

'Look after yourself, Tali, and thanks again for everything,' Nate whispered in her ear, as he hugged her before climbing into the car next to his new bride.

As she struggled to keep her composure, Nathalie recognised that Evan had moved his arm to circle her waist in support as a tear slipped down her cheek.

She dashed the tear away with her free hand. 'I'm okay.'

'Let's go inside, it's cold out here,' Evan replied.

'The party will be ending soon, I should find my parents.' Nathalie peered into the golden pool of light which spilled from the open door of the reception area out on to the driveway where she and Evan still stood.

'Have you got time for one dance?'

A shiver ran down her spine, and it wasn't

from the cold. The gentle warmth of Evan's hand on the small of her back and the musky scent of his cologne combined to send a tattoo of desire through her body.

'I don't know.' She licked lips that felt dry.

His eyes fixed on her face and she couldn't refuse when he continued to look at her the way she had always dreamed he would. The same way he had used to look at her.

'For old times' sake?' he murmured.

Dumbstruck, she nodded and he led her back inside.

The band switched to playing waltzes now the evening had almost drawn to a close. All around them, couples slowly circled the dance floor.

Nathalie's feet moved to the rhythm of the music, all her senses on maximum alert. She tried to scramble her brain into gear as they danced. They had always been well-matched as dance partners, and it was a rare pleasure to dance with a man who was taller than she was.

'Are you moving back to be near your family?' She knew Evan's mother and his sister still lived locally.

'Mum's not getting any younger and I've been offered a job here.' He twirled her around the corner of the dance floor. Her heartbeat quickened with the beat of the music.

'It sounds pretty definite, then?'

'I've some appointments to view properties tomorrow.'

The music stopped and the band leader started to make his announcements. Evan released her from his arms.

'Thank you for the dance.'

'My pleasure.' Nathalie shifted her feet. What was the matter with her? She hadn't felt so socially inept in years.

'I have to go. It was good to see you again. Could I give you a call sometime?'

'That sounds nice.' She struggled to sound cool and collected. Perhaps if she agreed to see him again, she would get some answers and maybe break this stupid spell he always seemed to cast over her.

'I'll be in touch.' He leaned forward and his lips brushed against her cheek to send heat into her skin.

It was only when her mother called to her from the edge of the dance floor that Nathalie realised Evan hadn't asked for her phone number.

She made her way across the room cursing herself for her stupidity at falling for his charm all over again.

'Could you come and help me see everyone off home?' Her mother asked.

'Of course.' She scanned the thinning crowd of guests. A little part of her half-hoped Evan might still be there and realise his mistake.

'Jerome's giving Evan a lift to his mother's. It was nice of him to call by.' Her mother moved to the door to say goodnight to some of Nate's employees.

Nathalie's heart sank. If he asked Jerome for her number she would be the subject of merciless and annoying teasing from her brothers. The problem with being the only girl in a family of brothers meant that any man who showed any kind of interest in her was subjected to the kind of interrogation the Spanish Inquisition would have taken pride in.

She walked across the hall to stand by her mother. The last little group of guests departed with hugs, kisses and pieces of wedding cake.

'You will still come to dinner tomorrow, won't you?' Her mother asked as she sank down onto a nearby armchair and slipped off her high-heeled patent leather shoes.

'If the offer's still good,' Nathalie teased.

'Good? You and Nate have always been so close, being twins. I don't want you to feel lonely now he's got Jenni.'

Nathalie sighed. She would miss being able to call Nate at any time now there was someone else to consider.

'I'll be fine.'

'Mmm.' Her mother didn't sound convinced.

'Really, Mum. I'm quite happy living on my own.' She knew her mother would love her to move back home, but Nathalie loved her little townhouse with its tiny garden and modern styling. She also valued her independence.

'Are you still seeing that young doctor you were dating?'

'I only saw him a couple of times.' She leaned on the top of her mother's chair and kissed her grey hair affectionately. 'It wasn't serious.'

'It never is, darling.'

Nathalie heard the note of reproof in her mother's voice.

'Mum, I told you I'm fine. I'm not like Nate, I like being single. I'm having fun.' She wondered if she told herself that often enough she would believe it.

'Oh sweetie, I just want you to be happy,

you know that.' Her mother squeezed her hand.

Evan watched from his mother's front door as the red tail lights of Jerome's car pulled away. It had been good to meet up with his old friends. It had been good to see Nathalie again. He turned the key and let himself into the darkened house, trying not to make a noise.

'Is that you, Evan?' His mother appeared from the kitchen with a china mug in her hand. She had changed into her nightwear.

'Yes, I thought you'd be in bed.'

'I just got up to make a drink and to check on Polly.' His mother smiled at him.

'Is she all right?' Evan's heart jumped. If anything had happened while he'd been gone, he would never forgive himself.

'She's fine. I heard her cough, but she's okay now,' his mother hastened to reassure him.

'I'll go up.'

Evan crept upstairs and pushed open the door to his daughter's room. His pulse settled when he saw her eyes were shut tight in sleep, her small face flushed and healthy in the soft glow of her nightlight.

Relieved, he closed the door and headed

for his room. Polly had been the both the joy and worry of his heart since the day she'd been born. Now that he had sole charge of her care, he worried about her ill health all the time.

Chapter Two

Evan watched as Polly ate her breakfast the next day. 'Are you sure you don't want some toast, Poll?'

Polly swallowed a small spoonful of cereal and shook her head. 'I'm full-up, Daddy.'

Evan frowned. Polly had such a little appetite, it was no wonder she looked so pale and slim. 'You'd better get your coat and shoes then, if you've finished. We're going to look at some houses today and see if we can find somewhere nice to live.'

'Somewhere I can have a pony?' Polly slid down from her seat, her small face hopeful.

'We'll see.' Evan helped her on with her coat before bending to fasten her shoes. He would willingly give his daughter the moon if it would make her well.

'Can Pookie come too?' Polly asked, as she reached for the tattered and much loved rag-doll that accompanied her everywhere she went.

'I suppose so,' Evan agreed. Since the divorce, Polly had clung on to her doll even more than before. He worried that she might miss her mother now he'd moved back to his hometown. Polly rarely talked about her, except at bedtime when she would sometimes ask God to bless her Mummy when she said her prayers.

Evan wondered how long it would take his ex-wife to remember she had a daughter and pay them a visit. Usually Laurel, his ex, only called when her modelling work became thin on the ground and she hoped to squeeze some money out of Evan.

He picked up the list of particulars from the estate agent and smiled at Polly, who waited with an eager expression by the front door, her beloved Pookie tucked under her arm. Maybe they'd find the perfect house today – a new home and a fresh start for them both.

Nathalie woke in the morning with the all-too-familiar spasms of pain in her stomach. She opened the drawer of her bedside cabinet for her tablets. At least the pain had held off till after the wedding. With any luck, if she swallowed the painkillers straight away, she should be all right for the remainder of the day.

She made her way downstairs to the

kitchen, massaging her stomach gently as she walked. Her calendar hung on the wall by the fridge, the hospital appointment ringed in red ink. Nathalie poured herself a glass of orange juice and swallowed her tablets. She already knew what her gynaecologist would say. They'd exhausted all the options medically, and a hysterectomy was the last solution. She padded through into the lounge and curled up on the settee, tucking her long, slim legs underneath her. Min, her cat, leapt up beside her, butting Nathalie's hip with a sleek brown head and demanding to be fussed.

'Oh Min, what am I going to do? I don't want this operation, but I've no life at the moment. I can't carry on the way I am now.'

The cat purred – a deep, low rumble of agreement against her thigh. Nathalie sighed and took another sip of her juice. If Evan hadn't left all those years ago, perhaps things would have been different. She might have been lucky and had a child of her own. Who knew? Now it was too late.

'You're right. I should stop feeling so sorry for myself.' Min stared at her with unblinking green eyes. Nathalie smiled and caressed her pet. At least she had her fur baby to keep her company. It was a waste of time to speculate on what might have been. She could only make plans from where she was now.

Nathalie felt better after an hour's rest, during which her tablets had started to relieve her discomfort. The weak winter sunshine warmed the windowsill where she'd placed Jenni's bridal bouquet. The scent of roses already filled the lounge with rich perfume.

She stroked one of the deep, red velvety petals. Whoever caught the bridal bouquet would be the next to be married – at least, that was the old wives' tale. Except getting married usually involved having children, forming a family.

'Oh, this is ridiculous! Nate gets married and I turn into a miserable old maid living alone with a cat.'

Min blinked at her from the sofa. Nathalie decided to take a walk down by the river to work off the unsettled feelings which had possessed her ever since she'd set eyes on Evan again.

Still tired after yesterday's festivities, she opted to dress for comfort in a soft warm tracksuit and padded pink jacket. Jerome always told her she looked like a marshmallow in her coat, but despite the sunshine, the February winds by the water's edge would be keen.

She bundled her long black hair under a knitted hat, pulled on her gloves and set off. Fortunately, it had been a dry winter. The river had stayed within its banks and the sun had tempted several people out onto the riverside walk near the new shopping centre.

After she'd walked for twenty minutes in the fresh air, Nathalie slowed her pace and dawdled along, watching couples out walking with their dogs and the families with small children who fed the ducks at the water's edge.

Absorbed in the scene around her, she startled when a familiar male voice called her name.

'Hello, Evan.' Her heart hammered in her chest as she realised her walk had probably given her pink cheeks and a red nose.

'I thought it was you. I couldn't be sure, though, in that coat.' He grinned at her.

'I was just walking.' She stopped in her tracks, annoyed with herself for feeling she had to justify her appearance to him.

'Looks nice and warm,' he said his face bland.

'It's a pretty colour,' a small voice added.

Nathalie tore her eyes away from Evan and realised he held the hand of a little girl whose wide blue eyes were just like his.

Her breath caught in her throat and her face must have revealed her bewilderment.

'Nathalie, this is my daughter, Polly. Polly, this is a friend of mine, Nathalie.' Evan performed the introductions as Polly continued to stare unblinkingly at her.

'Nice to meet you, Polly.' Nathalie forced her brain into gear and smiled at the little girl.

'We were on our way to view some houses, but one of the properties on the list has changed their minds about selling. We decided to come and see the ducks for half an hour before the next viewing,' Evan explained.

'We haven't got any duck food.' Polly gazed at the birds on the riverbank, her face wistful.

'Oh, we can fix that. If we walk up these steps to the café at the top, the owner keeps bags of scraps so children can feed the birds,' Nathalie said.

'Could we, Daddy? Please?' The child tugged at his hand.

Evan glanced at his watch. 'I suppose there's time. Can we buy you a coffee, Nathalie? You look pretty cold.'

Nathalie hesitated. Part of her wanted to spend more time with Evan, but the other more sensible part told her it was a bad idea. 'I am a bit chilly. Thank you, a coffee would be nice.'

She walked up the steps that led from the river bank alongside Polly and Evan, wondering why she'd agreed to a coffee. She'd opened her mouth fully intending to refuse his offer.

Evan collected two lidded cups and a bag of crusts from the hatch window of the small timber building and they made their way back to the water's edge.

Nathalie hid a smile behind her cup at the sight of Evan with Polly's doll tucked under his arm, supervising his excited daughter as she fed the greedy river birds.

It amused her to watch the confident, macho Evan she remembered turn to putty in the hands of a small child. She wondered how old Polly was. Four? Five? Six? The last number made her take too big a mouthful of coffee and she coughed as the hot fluid burned the back of her throat.

'Hey, are you alright?' Evan took his attention from Polly for a moment and his dark blue eyes met hers.

'I'm fine. I forgot this was so hot.' She felt the colour creep up her cheeks.

'Thanks for telling us about the café. Polly hasn't had so much fun in ages.' Evan tucked Polly's doll further under his arm and took a sip of his coffee.

'She seems a lovely little girl. How old is she?' Nathalie's heart bumped against her ribs, as she sensed the answer to her question might well give her the key to Evan's sudden disappearance from her life six years earlier.

Evan paused to take another sip of his coffee before he answered her. 'Polly will be six in a few months' time.' His eyes told Nathalie as much as his words.

'I see.' Pain twisted in her heart like a knife.

Evan frowned. 'No, you don't, Nathalie. We need to talk. There are things I need to explain.'

Nathalie finished her coffee and dropped the cup into a nearby rubbish bin. 'I really should be going. My parents are expecting me for lunch.' Much as she wanted answers, reasons why he'd run out on her she didn't think she could cope with hearing them right now.

Polly skipped back towards them, scrunching up her empty bread bag.

'Tali, let me call for you at your parents' house later. We could go for a drink.'

The use of her teenage nickname and the plea in Evan's voice made her relent. She felt torn between the need to know and fear of dredging up the pain of the past all over again.

'Okay. I'll be at Mum and Dad's till about six.' She wasn't sure she had done the right thing even as she agreed to meet him.

'I'll see you later.'

Polly put her rubbish in the bin before she took back her doll. She waved goodbye to Nathalie as she and her father turned to walk back towards the car park.

Nathalie made her way home deep in thought. Why had she agreed to meet Evan for a drink? Discussing the past would be more likely to reopen old wounds rather than providing her with the closure she craved. If she'd had his phone number, she would have been tempted to call and tell him she'd changed her mind.

By the time she reached her house, Nathalie realised she was late. She raced inside to tug off her hat and tidy her hair, pulling a face when she saw her pallid, make-up free face in the hall mirror.

Jerome opened the door when she arrived at her parents' house. 'Mum was just about to ring you.'

'I got held up.'

Jerome raised his eyebrows. Nathalie had a reputation for always being punctual, and so she knew her late arrival for lunch was bound to cause a stir.

'Must have been something important?' Jerome followed her along the hall as she took off her coat to hang it on the peg.

'Not really. I just got talking to someone and lost track of the time.' She shooed him away.

'Oh, so it was someone important, then.'

Nathalie glared at her brother as, with his shoulders shaking with laughter, he disappeared into the lounge.

'Is that you, Nathalie?' Her mother's voice called her from the kitchen. Her faint French accent still distinct even now, after all the years she'd spent living in England.

'Hi Mum, sorry I'm late.' She walked through into the large sunny room to find her mother bustling around the oven with a spoon in her hand.

'Be a love and strain those vegetables for me,' her mother directed, stirring the gravy as she spoke.

Nathalie did as her mother asked, straining broccoli and carrots into the china tureens ready to place on the dining table.

'Have you heard from Nate and Jenni?' she asked.

'Nate called from the cottage to say they had arrived safely.'

'The wedding went off well, I thought.'

Her mother gave her an enquiring glance. 'Yes, it was lovely. Your father had a nice talk with Miss Oakes at the reception.'

Nathalie flushed. Miss Oakes was her gynaecologist and a colleague of her father's at the hospital. She knew her surgeon wouldn't breach doctor-patient confidentiality, but her father must have detected that something was afoot.

'I have an appointment with her next week.' Her mother knew about her problems, but Nathalie had kept from her how bad the situation was, hoping not to worry her. Both her parents knew the probable outcome of her condition, but her mother had always been the more optimistic of the two.

'Do you want me to come with you?' her mother offered, as she poured gravy from a saucepan into the gravy boat.

'No, Mum. I'll be fine. I'm a big girl; I can

take care of myself.' Nathalie felt a twinge of guilt as she refused her offer. She would have liked some company, but she knew her mother wouldn't approve of her decision to press ahead with the operation.

'If you change your mind, let me know.' Her mother her gave her a quick hug.

'I will.' Nathalie picked up one of the tureens to carry into the dining room. She knew her mother still clung to the hope that some new drug would appear on the market which would solve Nathalie's problems and avoid the inevitable drastic step of surgery.

Once all the food was on the table and everyone was seated, Jerome resumed his probing about Nathalie's late arrival.

'Must have been an interesting someone you were talking to, Tali, to make you late for lunch.' He helped himself to a large spoonful of potatoes and grinned at her from across the table.

Nathalie gritted her teeth and smiled sweetly. Of all her brothers, Jerome was the one who always knew which button to press to wind her up. 'Not really.' She helped herself to some peas.

'Nice of Evan to drop by yesterday,' Jerome remarked.

'Yes, it was good to see him again. I heard

he planned to move back here,' her mother agreed.

Nathalie concentrated on her lunch. She knew Jerome was just trying to provoke her. He, like the rest of brothers, had remained unaware of how hurt she had been when Evan had left.

'How long has it been since he was last here?' her father asked.

'Six years, isn't it, Tali?' Jerome enquired.

Nathalie rested her knife down on her plate and picked up her glass to take a calming sip of wine. 'Must be.' She felt proud of her composure.

The conversation around the lunch table reminded her a little too keenly of her promise to go out with Evan that evening. What a stupid decision that had been on her part.

'You and Evan always seemed to get on so well, Nathalie. We must ask him over for dinner one evening.' Her father smiled at her.

'Um, well, actually, he's picking me up from here later.' She wriggled on her seat. 'We're going out for drinks.'

Jerome looked smug and Nathalie wrestled with a childish impulse to kick him under the table.

'You must have lots to catch up on. I heard in town that he has his little girl living with him.' Her mother took a sip of her wine.

'Yes. Polly.' The words were out of her mouth before she could stop herself.

Jerome helped himself to more potatoes. 'Did he tell you about his ex?'

Nathalie could tell by the look on his face that he had some interesting piece of information he longed to impart.

'Evan's private life isn't any of my business.' She felt determined not to give her brother the satisfaction of appearing interested.

'Then you won't want to know he was married to Laurel Hunter.'

Nathalie stared at her brother. He had to have made a mistake. Laurel Hunter was a big name in the fashion industry, appearing on all the covers of the glossy magazines. Nathalie had never read anything in the press about her having had a child.

'Laurel Hunter is Polly's mother? They don't look at all alike.'

Her parents looked at her in surprise. 'I wasn't aware you'd met Evan's little girl. When did you see her?' her mother asked.

'We met today, down by the river.' Nathalie blushed, kicking herself for blurting her thoughts out loud.

'Laurel wasn't famous when she met

Evan. In fact, she wasn't Laurel, she was just plain Laura then,' Jerome informed her.

Nathalie couldn't imagine the glossy blonde model the press had dubbed the Ice Princess being married to Evan, let alone being Polly's mother. Although she had wondered why Evan had custody of Polly and where Polly's mother was.

Nathalie's father collected the empty dinner plates to make room for dessert, and Nathalie helped her mother with the dishes. All the while, her mind tried to digest the information Jerome had given her.

She longed to find out more about Evan's life over the last few years. He had left her high and dry six years ago and now, not only was he back with a child, but his ex-wife was a glamorous model.

Evan strapped Polly back in the car with a sigh. They had viewed five houses and none of them seemed quite right. He knew what he wanted – a family home with three or four bedrooms and some land in a quiet spot with a good school nearby for Polly.

He wished he had someone with him to give their opinion. A female perspective when looking around the houses would be invaluable. It would also stave off the probing questions from the vendors about where his wife was, and why wasn't she viewing the properties with him.

Polly looked tired. Dark circles had formed under her eyes. He wanted to get her home before the air got too cold and triggered her coughing.

'We'd better take you back to Nanny's for tea. It's getting late.'

Polly cuddled her doll close to her. 'Are you going to see the lady from the river?' she asked.

'Do you mind?' Evan smiled at his daughter.

'I liked her. She knew where to get duck food.'

Evan grinned. Nathalie had scored major brownie points with Polly. The problem was he doubted if his own score was very high with Nathalie.

As he rang her parents' doorbell a couple of hours later, he wondered if he would ever manage to restore himself into Nathalie's good books.

From the way his heartbeat quickened when he looked into her dark blue eyes as she opened the door, he knew he wanted to be back on her good side, more than anything.

When he'd lost Nathalie, he'd made one of the biggest mistakes of his life. Now he'd met her again, it confirmed his feelings of regret. He owed it to her to try and put things right and give her the apology and explanation she deserved.

Chapter Three

Nathalie licked her dry lips. Being around Evan always made her nervous. The dark, serious look he gave her now made her feel even more nervous than usual.

'You'd better come in. I need to get my coat.' She stepped back into the hallway and Evan followed her inside. His wide frame filled the narrow entranceway. His proximity flustered her as she hurried along the hall to the coat stand, keen to put some space between them.

'Hey, Evan!' Jerome called through the open lounge door.

'Evening.' Evan greeted her parents and brother.

Relieved he wasn't still standing so near to her, Nathalie took advantage of his going into the lounge to tidy her hair and apply a fresh coat of lip-gloss.

She pulled on her marshmallow pink jacket and went through. 'I'm ready to go.' The evening ahead would be difficult enough without Jerome adding to her anxiety, so she was keen to leave as soon as possible.

'Have a nice time, dear,' her father said. 'And it's good to see you again, Evan.'

Nathalie followed Evan out of her parents' home, conscious of the curious eyes of her family watching them as they left. She hadn't felt so awkward since she'd been a teenager and had first started dating.

'Where are we going?'

Evan opened the door of his 4x4 for her. 'I thought we might go to The Lion, down by the river. It was always nice there.'

Anxiety swirled in Nathalie's stomach as she climbed into the passenger seat. 'It's been a long time since I went there.'

Not since you left, she thought. It had always been the pub she had thought of as being 'their place'. In the summer they had sat at tables near the water's edge and watched the boats glide up and down the river. In the winter they had sat inside near the inglenook fireplace, where the logs had crackled and popped as the flames flickered up the chimney and the horse brasses had twinkled in the firelight.

She sighed; knowing her perception of The Lion being special was hers alone. She doubted it had any such connotations for Evan.

Evan watched the range of emotions play across Nathalie's face. He'd suggested The Lion because it was familiar and all his memories of time spent there were pleasant. When he thought about it, most of his time spent there had been with Nathalie.

'For a minute in your parents' house I thought your dad was about to give us a curfew,' he joked.

Nathalie grinned. 'Me too. I think they forget sometimes that I'm not a teenager any more.'

'I take it you don't live at home?'

'No, I moved out a while ago, when my business took off and Nate moved out. I live nearer to town, as it's handy for the shop. None of us live there any more, although Jerome often calls around.'

Evan swung the car into the narrow country lane that led to the pub.

'This place doesn't look as if it's changed much,' he remarked as they pulled in to the car park. The white walls of the building were illuminated by yellow tinted flood-lights and a wisp of smoke curled from the chimney into the evening sky.

He jumped out of his seat and went to open the door for Nathalie.

48

'It seems quiet here tonight.' She looked around the almost deserted car park.

'I expect it'll get busy later.' Evan found himself reaching for Nathalie's hand as she climbed out of the car.

She ignored the gesture, and turned instead to lead the way through the small side gate to the entrance of the pub. He followed behind her, disappointed that she had snubbed his gesture and surprised by how much it stung.

The lounge was quiet. Another couple sat at a corner table sipping their drinks and an elderly man stood at the bar, deep in conversation with the landlord.

'What would you like to drink?' Evan asked. In the past he remembered Nathalie had always drunk soft drinks.

'Orange juice, please. I had wine at lunch and I need to drive home from Mum's later.'

Evan smiled as he collected the drinks and took a seat opposite Nathalie by the fireplace. Maybe some things didn't change.

Nathalie had taken off her jacket and hung it on the corner coat stand. In the soft light from the fire, her face appeared shadowed – almost mysterious. A frisson of electricity ran through his body. Nathalie was a very beautiful woman.

'I'm glad you agreed to come out with me.' He had thought when he'd asked her back at the river that she would refuse. In truth, he wouldn't have blamed her if she hadn't wanted to see him again. He owed Nathalie an apology – one that was long overdue.

'I guess I'm either a sucker for punishment or I want an explanation.' Her voice sounded brittle and her eyes were downcast, as if the wood grain of the table held some secret meaning.

Evan sighed. He felt like a heel. 'I never intended to hurt you, Tali.'

Her eyes snapped up to meet his. 'I never thought you did.' He wished he could believe her words but the pain on her face told a different story.

'I'd received a letter that morning from Laurel, when I last saw you. I'd seen her a few times when I was in London. I broke up with her a couple of months before you and I, you know, started to see each other as a couple.' He took a long pull of his beer. 'She said she was pregnant.'

'I knew you'd seen someone before we started to date, so why didn't you tell me?'

Evan raked his hand through his hair. 'I

didn't know if she was telling the truth or what her plans were. I had to go and see her.' He struggled to find the words to explain what his emotions had been like that fateful summer. How much he'd hoped that Laurel was mistaken.

'I see.' Nathalie's voice sounded cool.

'I intended to come back when I'd found out what was going on. I thought, hoped, she was lying.' God, how he'd hoped. He and Laurel had been over months before he'd started dating Nathalie.

'But she wasn't.'

He drew a deep breath. 'No, she wasn't.' Only the crackling of the wood as it shifted in the fireplace broke the silence between them. 'Believe me, Tali, I would have done anything to have made it not true.'

'So, you married her.' Nathalie's voice sounded so low he had to bend his head forward a little to catch what she said.

'She said she loved me and she was pregnant with my baby.' What else could he have done? He had a duty towards Laurel and his unborn child.

'I loved you.' Pain was evident in the sharp note which had entered Nathalie's voice. For a moment, hope flared in his heart that maybe she could come to feel that way again, but it was quenched by the unmistakable spark of fury in her eyes.

'Nathalie, I...' He wasn't sure what else he could say. Laurel had trapped him into a marriage he hadn't wanted, and while he bitterly regretted the way he had treated Nathalie, he would never regret his daughter.

'I thought we had something special back then, Evan. We'd talked, made plans together, then you kissed me goodbye after Maria's wedding and vanished.' She shook her head and a long, black tendril of hair fell loose across her cheek. 'I felt so stupid. No phone call, no letter, nothing. Then Jerome told me you'd settled in London and weren't coming back.' She glared at him.

'If I'd told you back then about Laurel, would it have made any difference?' he asked.

'I could have slugged you a good one.'

'That's fair, I would have deserved it. I behaved appallingly. I just convinced myself at the time that I had done the right thing.' He'd thought a clean break would be better for both of them. Except for Nathalie, it must have felt as if he'd simply lost interest and dumped her.

Nathalie drained the remainder of her drink and Evan noticed her hand shook as she placed the empty glass back down on the beer mat. 'Why is Polly with you now?'

Evan swished the dregs of his beer around in the bottom of his glass. 'The relationship was wrong from the start. We weren't in love. The only bond between us was the baby. Laurel – or Laura, as she was then – was just beginning to establish her career. She didn't want a child, but at the time it seemed all the major female celebrities were pregnant. It was fashionable.' He couldn't hide a grimace as he swallowed the rest of his drink.

'What happened?' Nathalie's eyes were dark in the dim light.

'She hated being pregnant. Once Polly was born, she abandoned any pretence of loving her once the cameras had stopped snapping at the various photo shoots she dragged Polly along to.' He paused as he relived the past, angry at the way he'd allowed himself and Polly to be used and manipulated.

'When did you leave?' Nathalie smoothed the stray curl of hair back from her face. Her expression looked blank again, telling him nothing of how she felt.

'Once Laurel's career began to take off, we were never together. She was travelling and working long hours, or so she said. I took care of Polly. We divorced six months ago.

Laurel liked the idea that I was still around, as a sort of financial safety net if her career nose-dived. But I finally got her to agree to a divorce.'

Nathalie blinked and he wondered if she had any idea what it had cost him to tell her all this.

'Poor Polly,' she murmured.

'Polly's health isn't very good. Ever since she was tiny she's had eczema and asthma. The eczema is better now she's older and her doctor is optimistic that she'll grow out of the asthma, but Laurel resented Polly's illness. It made her less photogenic.' Evan tried to keep the bitter note out of his voice. He found it hard to be civil to Laurel when she made one of her fleeting appearances in their lives. Her sporadic visits always brought Polly more sorrow than pleasure, but Laurel was still Polly's mother, so what could he do?

'That's terrible. Does Polly see her mother?' Nathalie's eyes widened with concern.

'She visits occasionally, usually if she wants something.' He grew aware of the increased volume of voices around them and realised the room had filled with customers whilst they had been talking. 'Would you like another drink?'

Nathalie looked at the empty glasses before them, then around at the busy room. 'No, I'm fine. Perhaps we ought to go.'

Evan took the empty glasses back to the bar. Nathalie had every right to be angry with him over the way he'd treated her. He should have got in touch with her sooner – explained about Laurel and the baby. He'd never thought of himself as being a coward and he prided himself on doing the right thing, but seeing the pain in Nathalie's eyes, he knew his pride had been misplaced.

Nathalie collected her coat and waited by the door for Evan to return. Her head buzzed with everything he'd told her. As she'd listened to Evan's story tonight, it hadn't given her the closure she'd hoped for. Instead it had reopened old wounds, just as she had feared it might.

Laurel might be a monster, but she had succeeded in giving Evan something Nathalie couldn't: a child. Nathalie knew from seeing them together that Evan loved Polly very much.

'Are you ready to go?' Evan's breath blew warm on the nape of her neck and her skin tingled at his closeness as he helped her on with her coat. She might still be angry with him, but when he stood so near her body played a traitor.

A refreshing blast of icy air hit her as she opened the door to go outside and she zipped her coat right up, snuggling into the puffy down as they crossed the car park to Evan's car. He made no move to take her hand this time making her shiver at the distance between them.

Evan unlocked the car to open the door for her. 'Polly thinks you're the bee's knees, by the way. Anyone who knows something as cool as where to find free duck food is a star in her eyes.'

Nathalie wriggled inside the Jeep, feeling slightly uncomfortable and waited for Evan to get in the driver's side. Polly had seemed a sweet little girl, but Nathalie hoped Evan didn't think she was a candidate to replace Laurel as a mother figure.

'It'll soon warm up in here.' He started the engine and waited for the frozen screen to clear. 'We talked a lot about me in there. What about you, Tali? You haven't felt the urge to get married or start a family?'

'I've been dating, but I suppose I haven't met the right person to settle down with yet.' Nathalie endeavoured to keep her voice light and concentrated on the half-moon of screen as it cleared in front of her.

'What about children?' Evan asked.

'Not for me,' she declared emphatically. Nathalie gripped the sides of her seat so hard her knuckles hurt. Maybe Evan wouldn't notice how much his probing had affected her.

'You'll change your mind one day,' Evan declared, his tone filled with confidence.

'The screen's cleared now, we'd better go.' Nathalie wanted to get home. She couldn't tell Evan the real reason she wasn't planning a family. It felt too personal, too painful, and she didn't want to see the look of pity in his eyes.

Too many people had made the same statement to her in the past – family, friends, and customers, all blithely assuring her that she'd have a baby of her own. All of them unaware of how much it hurt her each time she heard those words.

Evan gave her a puzzled glance but pulled out of the car park without any further comment.

'Drop me off at Mum's please. I need to collect my car.' She kept her eyes fixed on the windscreen in front of her. She didn't trust herself to look at him.

'Okay. Tali, I wish I could make things

right between us.'

'We're friends again now, aren't we?' She ignored the faint plea she thought she'd heard in his voice.

Silence hung heavy in the air for a moment before he answered her. 'Friends? Yes, I suppose so.' He drew the car to a halt outside her parents' home.

Nathalie blinked hard to keep back the tears that threatened. 'Friends it is, then.'

Evan clicked on the interior light and took her by surprise. She squeezed her eyes tight shut for a second as protection against the harsh yellow glare that filled the car.

'Are you alright, Tali?' Evan sounded concerned.

'I'm fine. The light was a bit bright, that's all.' She opened her eyes and forced a smile.

Evan studied her face and she longed to close her eyes again, afraid of what he might read there.

'I'm sorry. I should have warned you.'

'Well, I guess I'd better be going. Monday mornings are always busy at the shop. You know, people returning hire stuff.' She stopped talking, aware that her nerves had made her babble. She glanced towards her parents' house and wondered if they'd heard the car.

'I know this is going to sound cheeky, but I'd hoped to ask you a favour?' Evan's dark blue gaze was fixed on her face, pinning her to her seat.

'What kind of favour?' Nathalie's heart thumped. She hoped her voice didn't sound too breathless.

Evan sighed and looked away from her. 'You know Polly and I are house hunting? We viewed some places today and to be honest, I really could use a woman's perspective.'

'Why?' Nathalie knew she sounded blunt, but she had to protect herself. Being more than friends with Evan would mean her getting hurt all over again and she wasn't sure if asking her to view houses with him was a good idea.

'I'm okay looking at the structure, but imagining what it would be like decorated and whether it's suitable for Polly is pretty tricky. Plus, at every viewing today I got asked where my wife was and if she would be coming to view the house too.' He turned to face her again, a hopeful look on his face.

'Well, I–'

'Please, Tali.'

'Okay, I suppose I could come.' The words were out of her mouth before she could stop herself.

'I have some more appointments on Wednesday.'

'That would be fine as it's my closing day, but I already have something on in the morning. I'll be free after eleven.' She had almost said she had her hospital appointment that morning, but bit the words back just in time.

'I think they're all afternoon bookings. I really appreciate this, Nathalie.'

'What are friends for?' she replied and turned to open the car door.

'Wait!'

She felt the gentle pressure of his fingers on the sleeve of her coat. 'I don't have your address.'

Nathalie fumbled for her bag, struggling to ignore her body's response to Evan's casual touch. Being close to Evan was like being a diabetic in a sweet shop: she craved the sugar even though she knew it could kill her.

'Here.' She scribbled her address and phone number on a piece of paper torn from the back of her diary. 'Pick me up at lunch time.'

He tucked the paper securely inside his jacket pocket. 'Till Wednesday,' he said and leaning forward, he kissed her on the cheek.

Nathalie slid from her seat. Her knees shook as she forced herself to appear calm and collected. She walked over to her car, unlocked the door and waved to Evan as a sign that he could leave.

Once she was secure inside her car with her engine started, she watched the red taillights of Evan's Jeep disappear from view before she rested her trembling hands on the steering wheel.

Chapter Four

'Good grief, it's busy today.' Nathalie's assistant, Gemma, walked past with another bundle of hire suits in her arms.

Nathalie looked up from where she had been working in the back storeroom. She checked and tagged some of the suits, ready for the dry cleaner to collect. 'Tell me about it.'

Mondays were often busy with weekend hire returns, but this morning had been frantic. Nathalie's tummy rumbled with hunger and she glanced at her watch. Neither she nor Gemma had eaten and it was almost half past one.

'Go and have some lunch, Gemma. I'll finish these. It seems to have quietened down a little now, anyway.'

Her assistant didn't need to be told twice and soon deposited the clothes she carried on the table next to Nathalie. 'Do you want me to get you something?' Gemma slipped on her coat as she spoke.

'I'll pop out later, when you get back.'

Nathalie knew Gemma wanted to go and see her boyfriend, and Gemma's idea of a healthy diet wasn't the same as Nathalie's.

'Okay.'

The shop bell rang in the front of the shop and Gemma's face fell.

'It's alright, you go. I'll see to these.'

Gemma flashed a grateful smile and left via the back door, while Nathalie walked through from the staff area into the main body of the shop. A tall familiar figure stood by the window, gazing out on to the high street.

She faltered mid-stride before collecting her feelings. 'Hello again, Evan. I didn't expect to see you again before Wednesday.'

He turned to face her. 'I hadn't realised till I looked at your card that your shop was so near my new office. When I knew how close you were I thought I'd call in on my lunch break.'

Nathalie licked her lips. They had inexplicably dried when Evan had said he would be working so close at hand. 'I'm a little busy right now.' She flushed with embarrassment, realising too late how rude her statement sounded. She hadn't intended it that way.

Evan let his gaze travel around the empty shop. 'Mmm, so I see.'

'I mean, my assistant has just gone for her break, so I'm on my own.' Her inability to conquer her feelings irritated her, and even more annoying was her sudden inability to have a normal, polite conversation.

Nevertheless, Evan's brow cleared. 'Have you had any lunch yourself yet?'

'Believe it or not, we haven't stopped all morning.' Nathalie bent to straighten the hem of a gown on a nearby display dummy, glad of the opportunity to dodge Evan's piercing gaze for a moment.

'It's almost two now,' he pointed out. 'Let me go and get you something to eat.'

'No, really, I'll have something when Gemma gets back.' Nathalie straightened up relieved the heat seemed to have died down from her cheeks.

'You never did eat properly.' He smiled at her.

'Yes, well, you sound like Mum.'

He used to tease her like this before, when he had been her brothers' friend and she'd been the annoying kid sister. It was an old joke between them and as he smiled at her now, with the endearing laughter lines crinkling the corners of his eyes, her heart raced.

'Okay, well, I'd better get back to the office. I'll see you on Wednesday.'

The shop bell pinged and a customer walked in. Evan raised his hand in a brief goodbye and slipped out of the door.

Nathalie was immersed in helping a nervous bride-to-be try on various tiaras and veils when Gemma arrived.

'There's a parcel for you in the back,' she murmured to Nathalie.

'Parcel?' She wasn't expecting a delivery.

'A really handsome guy handed it to me as I came in through the back door. It looks like lunch to me. He gave me a note.' She passed Nathalie a slip of paper.

Gemma took over helping the customer while Nathalie read the note.

'Enjoy your dinner, Mum.'

Nathalie grinned. She checked that Gemma was happy to take over with her customer and went through to the kitchen.

'Bagels, cream cheese and salmon.' She lifted out the contents of the bag and found herself a plate, still smiling to herself.

Evan walked back to his office, deep in thought. His delivery of lunch to Nathalie reminded him of the times he and her brother had dropped food off to her at work from her mother. Nathalie had worked at numerous jobs to fund her way through college and

then to raise money for her business.

Nathalie worked harder than anyone he knew except possibly Nate, her twin. Yet she was such a bundle of contradictions. She worked herself into the ground forgetting to look after herself, but still ran around after everyone else taking care of them.

Jerome sat waiting on one of the leather chesterfield sofas in the lobby when Evan arrived back at the office. 'Your secretary said you'd be here soon. I thought I'd call in and see how you're settling back in to town.'

'Come through to the office. I've just taken your sister some lunch.'

Jerome grinned and followed Evan inside the oak panelled room. 'I'm surprised she's speaking to you.' He glanced around Evan's office. 'Nice place.'

'Yeah, it's not bad.' He motioned to Jerome to sit down on a carved wooden chair.

'So, you told Nathalie about Laurel and Polly?'

Evan took a seat behind his large oak desk. 'I told her everything.'

Jerome raised his eyebrows in mild surprise. 'It hit her hard when you disappeared. I know you had your reasons, but I don't want to see her get hurt again. You might be my mate, but Tali's my sister – you know

66

what I'm saying?'

Evan looked at Jerome's sombre face. 'I know.' He knew just what Jerome meant. From the bottom of his heart, he wished he'd handled the situation with Laurel differently. He wished he'd told Nathalie about Polly when he'd first had the letter.

But the past was the past, and he couldn't alter what had already happened. 'We can still be friends,' he'd told her, though the attraction that had burnt so brightly between them in the past was still as strong, at least on his part. It made him wonder if 'being friends' would turn out be a lot harder to cope with than he'd imagined.

'Listen, I can see you must be busy blowing the dust off all those wills and things, so I'll push off. I'll call you for golf at the weekend.'

Evan smiled. Jerome always poked fun at his profession as a solicitor. 'I'll look forward to it, old boy,' he teased, in a fake upper-class drawl.

'Are you going to tell me who he is,' was the first thing Gemma asked when Nathalie rejoined her on the shop floor. The nervous bride-to-be had gone and Gemma was busy replacing tiaras on the display stand.

'Evan? He's an old friend.'

'Mmm, I wouldn't mind an old friend who looked like that. He's certainly put a smile on your face.' Gemma stepped back to admire her handiwork on the display.

'Really, he's just a friend.' Nathalie frowned at Gemma in mock severity.

'Well, come on, spill! Where did you meet him and how come someone so hunky is just a friend?'

'He's a friend of Jerome's. I've known him for years. We dated for a short time ages ago, then he moved away.' Nathalie fiddled with a small stack of business cards next to the till.

'Don't tell me he's married? All the good ones are married.' Gemma groaned. 'Except Carl, of course,' she added hastily, referring to her own boyfriend.

'He's divorced.' Nathalie tapped the edges of the cards on the counter, lining them up in a neat pile.

'That's good. Well, it isn't for him, but – oh, you know what I mean.' Gemma shot her a questioning glance. 'It is good, isn't it? I mean, you can see he's interested in you, surely.'

Nathalie felt Gemma's trusting brown eyes bore into her. 'I don't know. There's a lot of history between us, not all of it good. He's got a little girl, as well.' She picked up the top card and folded it into little pleats. She wasn't sure if he was interested or, for that matter, if she even wanted him to be. She'd had her heart broken by Evan once before.

'Single parent, huh? Does he have custody?' Gemma's face was alive with curiosity.

Nathalie nodded. 'Polly lives with Evan. He's looking to buy a house now he's moved back to town.' Nathalie didn't say anymore, since she wasn't sure if the identity of Polly's mother was common knowledge.

'It sounds as if we'll be seeing more of him,' Gemma observed.

'Maybe. His office isn't far away, that's how come he dropped by.' Nathalie stared at the tiny cardboard fan she held with unseeing eyes.

'I think he'd have found an excuse to drop by even if he'd been five miles away.' Gemma tweaked the card from Nathalie's hand. 'Although it might be kinder on your business cards if he didn't drop in very often.' She laughed.

'I told you, we're just friends.' Nathalie shook her head as her assistant walked off towards the fitting rooms, still laughing.

The afternoon bought in a flurry of customers and meant Nathalie was late closing the shop. She sent Gemma home earlier when her boyfriend had called in to give her a ride home.

Nathalie grimaced as she locked the shop door and pressed the button to lower the security grill. The hateful familiar stomach cramps, which had been held at bay all day by her medication, began to make themselves known again.

She rubbed her abdomen discreetly as she waited for the grill to click into place.

'Can we give you a ride home?'

Evan's car had pulled to the kerb behind her and he hailed her through the open driver's window. She could see Polly admiring the beautiful gowns in the window through the squares of the security mesh.

'I'm okay, thanks. I don't live very far from here, so I usually walk home.' She set the alarm and locked down the little door that covered the buttons.

'Are you always this late finishing? Polly and I have been to see her new school and we called to pick up some more house details on our way home.'

'I sometimes finish earlier, but it's been a busy day. Hello Polly.' Nathalie smiled at the little girl on the back seat, who still appeared to be engrossed by the dresses sparkling and twinkling under the halogen lights in the shop window.

'Is this your shop?' she asked.

Evan smiled at the rapturous expression on his daughter's pale face.

'Yes, it's mine.' Nathalie's heart melted at the tenderness in Evan's eyes as he looked at his child.

'The dresses are so beautiful! Like the ones princesses wear,' Polly said breathlessly.

A plop of icy water hit Nathalie's cheek as the heavens opened and raindrops began to pelt down on her like silver pennies.

'Get in the car,' Evan commanded as he opened the passenger door for her. Faced with a choice of getting soaked or a short, dry ride home, Nathalie obeyed her first instinct and jumped in. It seemed as if even the elements were determined to conspire against her.

'We were on our way to get something to eat. Would you like to join us?' Evan asked.

'I don't know. I mean, you and Polly probably have plans.' Nathalie heard herself falter. She needed to take some more of her tablets but she couldn't very well do that in plain view. She hesitated, trying to decide what to say.

'Daddy promised we could go somewhere with a play area,' Polly said.

Evan smiled an apology at Nathalie. 'There's a family pub just on the edge of town that has a ball-pit. It's nicer than it sounds, I promise.'

'It'll be fun. You can tell me about the pretty dresses.' Polly's face looked wistful.

'So long as I don't have to get in the ball-pit.' Much to her surprise Nathalie heard herself agree.

'It's okay. You and I can sit in the grown-up area.' Evan set the wipers in motion and pulled away from the kerb.

Nathalie watched the blades swish back and forth in front of her, wondering just what she'd let herself in for. An inn with play facilities would usually be the last place she would want to spend her spare time. Being surrounded by parents and children while she watched everyone play happy families was too painful.

'You've gone quiet,' Evan observed a few minutes later.

'Sorry, I'm a bit tired.' She did feel tired, but being with Evan made her feel unsure of herself. Nathalie wasn't the kind of person to feel unsure of anything. Normally she was confident and outgoing, more than capable of holding her own in any situation. Except it seemed where Evan was concerned.

'I appreciate you coming with us.' Evan lowered his voice and glanced at his daughter in the rear view mirror. 'Polly doesn't take to people easily, but she seems to like you. I think it helps that she loves princesses and fairy tales. Her favourite thing at the moment is dressing her dolls in wedding dresses.'

'Oh.' Nathalie chewed her lower lip. She felt flattered that Polly liked her, but her inner sense distrusted the way Evan seemed so ready to slot her into a nurturing role for his daughter.

'Here we are.' Evan swung the car into the car park and found a free space as close to the doors as he could get. Rain still pelted down, bouncing off the bonnet and running in streams down the windscreen.

'You go on in, Tali. I'll get Polly.' Evan turned up the collar on his dark wool jacket and undid his seatbelt.

Nathalie clutched her bag to her and, jumping down from the car, made a dash for the entrance. Evan followed, hot on her heels with Polly and her doll in his arms.

'Whew, it's really coming down.' Evan

73

joined Nathalie inside the entrance and lowered Polly carefully to her feet.

Polly clutched her doll to her chest and coughed. Her little body shook with the violence of the fit. Evan bent to soothe his daughter until the coughs that racked her thin doll-like frame came to an end.

Nathalie felt helpless as she stood to the side, watching Evan calm and care for his child. She was filled with sympathy for Polly as Evan patiently helped her take a puff from the inhaler he produced from her little pink backpack.

'Do you feel okay now, Poll?' Evan knelt so that his face was level with his daughter's, uncaring of any effects the damp carpet might have on the trousers of his expensive-looking suit.

Polly nodded; tendrils of blonde hair tumbled free from her ponytail as she did so. Evan got to his feet, brushing the knees of his trousers as he stood up.

'We'd better move further inside. We're blocking the doorway.' He placed a gentle hand on Polly's shoulder and Nathalie walked with them into the restaurant area.

Once they were seated and Evan was satisfied that Polly felt better, he went to order drinks from the bar. Nathalie rummaged in her bag for her tablets so she could take them once Evan returned with her orange juice.

'Do you have medicine, too?' Polly's fixed her gaze on the packet in Nathalie' s hand.

'Yes, I have to take medicine like you.' Nathalie wasn't sure how to answer Polly, but decided it would probably be best to stick to a simple explanation.

'I have a puffer. Do you have a puffer?'

'No, I have to take tablets instead.' Nathalie smiled at the look on Polly's small face.

'Yuck! I don't like medicine. Daddy gives me pink medicine from the doctor. He says it tastes like strawberries but it doesn't really.' Polly pulled a face to show Nathalie just how bad the medicine tasted.

'Polly!' Evan slid a tray of drinks onto the table and stared in amazement at his daughter's strange expression.

'She was telling me about the lovely medicine you make her take,' Nathalie explained.

'Mmm, I bet she didn't use the word 'lovely'. Last time she had to take some I ended up wearing more than the amount she swallowed.' Evan ruffled Polly's hair.

'So what do you two beautiful ladies want for dinner?'

Nathalie slipped her tablets into her mouth

and swallowed them with a sip of juice while Evan helped Polly study the menu.

'I want chicken nuggets, please,' Polly didn't hesitate.

'Are you sure you wouldn't like a proper dinner, Poll?' Evan frowned.

Nathalie looked at Polly's face and guessed that this discussion had taken place more than once. As someone who'd been a skinny child herself, she had a certain amount of sympathy for Polly, but she could also emphasize with Evan. Polly's fragile health must be a constant source of worry to him.

'I'll have a jacket potato with cheese and beans, please. I've got to leave room for a pudding.' Nathalie snapped her menu shut and winked at Polly, who giggled. 'Well, we do get pudding if we eat all of our dinner, don't we?' Nathalie looked hard at Evan.

'I suppose so. But I want to see it all gone.' He caught on and directed his answer at Nathalie, causing Polly to giggle even harder until she broke off into a small cough.

Evan waited until Polly had recovered before he returned to the bar to order the food.

'Do you wear princess dresses?' Polly regarded Nathalie with solemn eyes over the rim of her glass.

'I wore one on Saturday.' Nathalie decided Polly was obviously a child who liked to ask questions.

'Cool! Did you go to a ball and dance with a prince?'

Nathalie laughed. 'It was my brother's wedding and I danced with your daddy.'

Polly took a long slurp of juice, with the appearance of considering Nathalie's answer. 'Daddy's not a prince.'

'Who says I'm not a prince?' Evan rejoined them. 'I might be a prince in disguise, and then you, being my daughter would be Princess Polly.'

Nathalie joined in with Polly's laughter and the next hour flew past as the two of them teased Evan over dinner. She was relieved to see that Polly ate all of her dinner and even managed some ice-cream for her pudding.

'I think we'd better go home.' Evan finished the last of his daughter's dessert while Polly yawned and snuggled her doll.

'I'm not tired, Daddy,' she said, blinking heavily.

'I am, though, and my cat will wonder where I am.' Nathalie stood up ready to collect her coat from the wooden stand behind Evan's seat.

'Is it a girl cat or a boy cat?' Polly asked as her father helped Nathalie with her jacket.

'A girl, of course.' Nathalie was conscious of Evan's fingers brushing against the nape of her neck as he straightened her collar for her. At least her fitted jacket flattered her figure a little better than her marshmallow coat. Not that it mattered what she wore, since she wasn't out to impress Evan at all, she told herself.

'When we find a new house I'm going to have a pony.' Polly picked up her doll and her backpack.

Nathalie felt relieved when Evan went to help Polly with her coat, having him so close to her felt too intimate and disturbing to her senses. When he was around, it was as if she found herself slipping into teenage mode.

The evening had been fun, but she had the worrying feeling that she might have let her guard down a little too much where Evan and his daughter were concerned. Polly was a sweet little girl and her Daddy was much too handsome for Nathalie's peace of mind.

Chapter Five

Polly fell asleep in her car seat before they were even five minutes into the journey.

'I'll drop you off at home, Tali,' Evan said, his voice low.

'Thank you. She's very tired, isn't she?' Nathalie peeked in the rear view mirror at the sleeping child. Polly's blonde curls were tumbled about her face and pale blue smudges were beneath her closed eyes.

'Poll gets tired easily but she doesn't sleep very well when she's in bed. I'm hoping she'll be tired enough now to go through the night.'

'It must be hard bringing her up alone.' As soon as she'd spoken the words aloud, she wished she could take them back. Her voice sounded too wistful, and she hoped Evan hadn't picked up on it.

'Mum helps since I've been back at home, but to be honest, things have been better since Laurel left.' Evan stopped the car for a red light. 'I can't believe you've changed your mind about wanting a family. You always loved kids.'

Pain shot through Nathalie's abdomen and it took her till the lights changed back to green before she could reply. 'I like children, but its different having your own. You know that from having Polly. It's just not for me.' She tried to keep her tone light. When she'd dated Evan before, they'd talked about children. Her heart clenched at the memory.

'You've never been someone to duck responsibility.' Evan frowned.

'Look, Evan, can we just drop this please? I'm not cut out to be a mum, okay? I'm free and single and that's how I like it.' She snapped the words out and turned her head to look out of the side window so he couldn't see her face. She knew if he did her expression would give her away.

Evan pulled to a halt in front of her townhouse a few minutes later. 'I'm sorry. Your private life is none of my business.' His voice sounded stiff.

'Thank you for lunch and for a nice evening.' Nathalie had her hand ready on the door handle, poised for flight. Evan's expression was hard to read in the dimly-lit interior of the car.

'I guess I'll see you on Wednesday then,' he said, his words a statement rather than a query, as if he suspected she might try to back out. 'Thanks for taking the time to play with Polly tonight.'

'I like Polly, she's a lovely child.' Nathalie was sincere. She did like Evan's daughter very much, but if he thought he could arrive back in Nathalie's life after a six year absence and expect...

What did he expect? Tiredness washed over her and the cramps in her stomach only served to muddle her thought processes further. She shook her head a little to clear the fuzziness.

'Are you alright?' Evan leaned closer to her.

'I'm fine. It's been a long day.' She couldn't bring herself to look at him.

'If you're sure?' He opened the door for her. His hand covered hers with unexpected warmth.

'I have to go. You need to take Polly home.' Nathalie heard herself gabble, but Evan's hand still lingered over hers.

'Goodnight then, Tali.' His lips brushed her cheek and she half clambered and half fell out of his car. The impression of where his lips had touched her skin tingled like fire.

She hurried up the steps to her front door, fumbling in her bag for the key. Only when she had shut the door firmly behind her did she hear Evan drive away.

Evan watched as Nathalie disappeared from view inside her house. He could have sworn when he'd covered her hand with his in order to open the car door, he'd felt her fingers tremble against his palm.

After checking on Polly, who continued to sleep soundly in the back of the car, he pulled off into the traffic. He couldn't recall the Nathalie he remembered from six years ago ever looking as sad and vulnerable as when the Nathalie of today had left his car moments earlier.

While he'd been away, Jerome had kept him up to speed with snippets of information about Nathalie and the rest of the family. As such, he knew a little about what had happened in her life, but nothing to prepare him for the hurt he'd seen on her face when he'd asked her about starting a family of her own.

Something had changed in Nathalie's life while he'd been away, and while he was prepared to own a portion of the blame for the hurt he'd caused her, there had to be something else going on. Something he didn't know about. Whatever the mystery was, he was determined to solve it.

Evan came to a halt in front of his mother's home and Polly stirred a little in her car seat.

The Tali he remembered was a confident, feisty young woman who loved life and romance. A girl who'd once confided her hopes and dreams of marriage and a family to him. A girl who'd shared his dreams. Now all that had changed.

On the surface Nathalie appeared to be the same breezy woman he recalled, but several times during the course of the evening he had felt as if he were walking on eggshells. It was as if the real Tali lay hidden behind a public façade, carefully constructed to hide her innermost feelings. Deep in thought, Evan turned off the engine and climbed out ready to carry his sleepy daughter into the house.

'Where's Nathalie?' Polly demanded in a grumpy voice as he lifted her from her seat.

'She's gone home, sweetheart.' Evan locked the car and carried Polly up the path to the house.

'I wanted to show her my Princess doll.' Polly pouted and hugged Pookie close as Evan set her on her feet in the hallway.

'You can show her some other time,' Evan said as he began to undo the buttons on her coat.

'But she promised to see my dolls.'

Evan sighed. 'Then she'll see them another day. Nathalie always keeps her promises.'

Polly appeared mollified and allowed her father to remove her coat and shoes. Evan smiled as he escorted Polly upstairs to get her washed and changed for bed. He remembered the time Nathalie had promised to walk the neighbours' dog for them while they'd been away. The dog had been a huge, unruly mutt that on the first outing, had dragged Nathalie for miles over the surrounding fields. She limped home covered in mud and missing a shoe.

Most girls he knew would have cried off after that, but Nathalie had stuck it out, even taking the animal treats she'd bought out of her own money because she'd given her word that she would look after the dog.

She'd also given her word to go house-hunting with him, and although he suspected she might be looking forward to accompanying him about as much as she'd enjoyed walking that dog, he had no doubts about her keeping her promise.

After she'd heard Evan drive away from the house, Nathalie unfastened her damp jacket with trembling fingers. She sat down on a nearby armchair and held her head in despair. 'Oh Min, this is hopeless. What am I going to do? Polly is so sweet and Evan is...' What was Evan?

The cat raised her neat head from her position on the sofa to fix Nathalie with a solemn green-eyed gaze.

Nathalie sighed. Her thoughts kept taking her down avenues she didn't feel ready to explore. Her abdomen cramped with pains and she rubbed her hand across her stomach to ease the discomfort. 'I need to take a bath and see if this pain will go.'

The cat continued to clean her front paws.

'Okay, I'm talking to you, Minnie!' Nathalie reproved as she walked across the lounge and scooped Min up into her arms. She buried her face in the cat's soft fur and felt a deep rumble of contentment against her cheek.

Nathalie walked into the kitchen and set Min down on the floor, before taking some milk from the fridge, and pouring some into the cat's bowl. Min twined herself in between Nathalie's legs, meowing with excitement, then dove straight in for a drink.

The circled date on the calendar caught Nathalie's attention and she placed a protective hand on her stomach. Wednesday would bring more than one difficult moment for her.

'You're very quiet today,' Gemma observed the next morning as she helped Nathalie re-hang bridal gowns after the customer who had tried them on had left.

'Am I? Sorry, Gemma. I've a lot on my mind.'

'Mmm. Is one of the things on your mind six-foot-two with blue eyes and dark blond hair?' Gemma teased.

'You are incorrigible!' Nathalie shook her head.

'I notice you're not denying it.' Gemma slid a protective cover over a gown.

'There's nothing to deny.'

'He bought you dinner.'

'He bought me supper as well,' Nathalie admitted. She smiled at Gemma's startled expression.

'Oh, come on, Tali! You can't throw me a teaser like that and not give me the details.' Gemma followed her into the back store area.

'There's not a lot to tell.'

Gemma gave a snort of disbelief.

Nathalie filled the kettle and got two mugs down from the cupboard. 'I was locking up last night and Evan passed by as it started raining. He had Polly with him and we went for a meal at the family pub on the edge of town.'

'Not your average romantic candlelit dinner for you two, then.' Gemma sounded wistful.

'I told you. We're not on those kinds of terms.' Nathalie spooned coffee into the mugs.

'You didn't tell me why you split up with him before?'

Nathalie's hand shook a little as she added the boiling water. 'It's a bit complicated.'

'Because of Polly?' Gemma's warm, brown eyes were dark with sympathy. She was one of the few people who knew about Nathalie's medical problems. As she worked so closely with Nathalie, it would have been impossible for Gemma not to notice the days when Nathalie had been in pain or had been forced to leave work to attend medical appointments.

'A little bit, I suppose,' Nathalie admitted as she stirred the drinks.

'I would have thought...' Gemma bit back on her words.

'That if I got together with Evan I would be delighted to have Polly as a step-daughter as I can't have children of my own?' Nathalie completed the sentence.

Gemma looked stricken.

Nathalie took a sip of her coffee. She didn't mean to snap at her assistant. At least Gemma had been bold enough to attempt to put into words an idea which she suspected many people would have had if they had been aware of her condition.

'I'm sorry.' Gemma bit her lower lip.

'No, I'm sorry. Anything to do with Evan and I turn into someone I don't like very much. I shouldn't have snapped.'

'You really like him, don't you?' Gemma picked up her own mug and cradled it thoughtfully.

'He hurt me a lot last time, Gemma. I just don't know if I can risk that again.' Nathalie stared into her mug as if she expected to see the answer to her dilemma floating on the pale brown surface of the coffee.

The shop bell jangled and Gemma put her mug down on the table. 'Only you can decide if he deserves a second chance, but we've worked together for three years now and I've never seen a man have this kind of impact on you.' Then she walked out in to the shop and began to talk to someone.

Nathalie took another sip of coffee and

tried to collect her thoughts. It was crazy to start thinking so far ahead. Evan had only just re-entered her life. She wasn't even sure of his intentions towards her.

'Certainly, I'll see if she's free,' Gemma said, her voice a little louder. 'Sorry, it's Karen Gillespie.' Gemma's face registered her distaste for the customer in the shop as she reappeared.

Nathalie shared her assistant's dislike of Karen. A former classmate of Nathalie's, Karen was in the throes of planning her third wedding and her plans altered almost daily, driving both Nathalie and Gemma round the bend.

Nathalie took another fortifying sip of coffee and followed Gemma out onto the shop floor.

'Nathalie, darling!' Karen swooped over in a cloud of strong perfume to plant air kisses on Nathalie's cheeks.

'Hello, Karen. What can we do for you today?'

Karen opened her bag and produced her journal of wedding plans. 'I had a thought about the wedding favours. Sugared almonds are so passé, and I wondered if handmade chocolate truffles might be better.'

'Fine, I'm sure that won't be a problem.'

Nathalie waited for Karen to work her way through a list of alterations and was surprised to see her return the book to her bag.

'I saw Evan Davies the other day.' Karen smiled at Nathalie. 'You and he were rather close at one time, weren't you?'

Nathalie pinned a smile to her face, Karen had always been nosy. 'Evan's an old friend. It'll be nice to have him back in town.'

'You know he was married to Laurel Hunter?' Karen delivered the information with the air of someone who had uncovered a state secret.

Nathalie felt the tension build in her jaw as she tried to keep her smile in place. 'Oh yes, I believe it's common knowledge.' She wasn't certain that it was, but knew it would wipe the smirk off Karen's immaculately made-up face if it looked like she didn't have the inside track.

'He has custody of the child, doesn't he? It's a very strange affair in my opinion. The mother nearly always gets custody.' Karen sniffed.

'I'm sure they have their reasons for Polly being in Evan's care.' Nathalie glanced around to look for Gemma, hoping she might come to the rescue. She had, however, disappeared back into the store room.

'Have you seen them, then?' Karen fingered the edge of a diamante spangled veil with ill-disguised disinterest.

'Evan came to Nate's wedding reception.' Nathalie itched to smack Karen's pointy-nailed fingers away from the delicate lace.

'I didn't realise you'd stayed in touch. Didn't he disappear and leave you in the lurch before?'

'You shouldn't believe everything you hear. Like I said, we're old friends.' Nathalie had no intention of letting on to Karen that she hadn't even known Evan would be at the reception. Karen was one of the biggest gossip-mongers in town.

'Well, when you see him next remember me to him, won't you? Perhaps you could bring him to my wedding rehearsal?' Karen suggested.

Nathalie thought she would rather stick forks in her eyeballs, but she continued to smile at her customer. 'If I see him, I'll ask.' She crossed her fingers surreptitiously behind her back.

'Marvellous, darling. Well, I'd better be getting along.' Karen hitched her bag onto her shoulder and patted her auburn hair into place.

'I'll sort out the wedding favours for you

and call to confirm.'

Karen looked blank for a moment. 'Oh yes, of course. That'll be super. Bye, then.'

The shop door closed behind Karen and Nathalie's shoulders sagged with relief.

'Is it safe to come out?' Gemma slipped back through the curtains.

'Yes, she's gone.'

'Here's a fresh coffee. I thought you'd need it.'

'I need a brandy after I've seen Karen.' Nathalie accepted the mug from Gemma with a grateful sigh.

'What did she want this time?'

'I'm not quite sure. She said she wanted to change the wedding favours, but she was more intent on trying to dig up information on Evan. Oh, and she wants me to invite him to her wedding rehearsal.' Nathalie pulled a face.

'Why?' Gemma looked baffled.

Nathalie shrugged. 'You know I told you Evan's ex-wife was Laurel Hunter? Well, Karen likes to think she's the queen bee of every social event in town, doesn't she? You can bet she'd be on to the press like lightning if Evan went to the rehearsal just so she could make the society column.'

'Her whole wedding is one big drama. No

one else would turn their rehearsal into a lunch party except Karen. Anyway seeing as she's on her third husband, you'd think she'd know the words by now.' Gemma pulled a sour face.

'Ouch, you really don't like her, do you?' Nathalie tried to look disapproving but couldn't hide her smile.

'Does it show?' Gemma laughed. 'I take it you're not planning on asking Evan to go with you to the rehearsal then?'

'What do you think?'

Gemma shook her head and collected Nathalie's empty mug from her hand ready to take into the back room. 'At least Karen's wedding is just a couple of weeks away. After that, we won't have to see her again. Until number four comes along, of course.'

Nathalie smiled ruefully as Gemma whisked away. Karen might be a pain in the neck, but she was a good customer when it came to spending money. And because of her social connections, she sent Nathalie lots of very well-heeled customers.

Compared to the impending appointment at the hospital the next day however, Karen's wedding wasn't at the top of Nathalie's list of priorities.

Once the shop had closed for the day and

she'd said goodnight to Gemma, Nathalie made her way home with a heavy heart, tomorrow's appointments preying on her mind. Light drizzle fell from a steel grey sky and water dripped miserably from the bare branches of the trees that lined the streets on her route home.

She heard the phone ring as she unlocked her front door. Min rushed to greet her, twining round her legs with loud purrs as Nathalie struggled into the lounge to answer it. She snatched the handset up in time, and tried to ignore the inconvenient flicker of hope that it would be Evan's voice on the other end.

Chapter Six

The relentless chirp of the alarm clock roused Nathalie from a deep sleep. It had taken her a long time to fall asleep the previous night. Her mother's phone call offering to accompany her to the appointment with the gynaecologist, though well-intentioned, had stirred a well of mixed emotions for Nathalie.

She lay still for a moment, enjoying a few minutes of peace and quiet before going for a shower. The appointment weighed heavy on her mind. Part of her dreaded hearing that there was nothing more that could be done unless she accepted surgery. On the other hand, she longed to be free of pain – to lead a life independent of painkillers and cramps.

She slipped out of bed and put on her slippers before heading for the kitchen. Min padded along behind her, mewing with delight at the prospect of her regular morning bowl of milk.

'Big day today, Min.'

Min sat on her haunches and stared at Nathalie with big green eyes. Nathalie sighed as she poured some milk into Min's china bowl. If she were being honest with herself, she wasn't sure if it was just the appointment at the hospital that bothered her.

She finished her coffee and swallowed more tablets. Evan was due to call round at lunchtime, giving her time to compose herself and digest whatever news her consultant might have for her.

When Nathalie emerged from the hospital later that morning, she knew her eyes had to be pink from tears, but she felt as though a weight had been lifted from her shoulders. The decision was made and she had agreed an operation date for the autumn with her surgeon.

She glanced at her watch and realised she would need to hurry if she were to make it back home in time to change her clothes. She'd worn a suit for her appointment, subconsciously hoping a smart appearance would give her a better outcome. Now she wanted to change into a more casual and comfortable pair of jeans and sweater in order to accompany Evan on his house hunt.

An accident on the ring road slowed traffic

to a crawl. She pulled to a halt outside her house to find Evan's car already at the kerb. Nathalie glanced at her reflection in the rear view mirror to check that the redness had faded from her eyes before she got out of the car.

'Am I too early?' Evan stood by his car. She felt his gaze take in her formal attire. 'You look very smart.'

'Thank you. I'm sorry, I got held up at my appointment. The traffic was awful. Do you mind if I go and change? I'll feel a bit over-dressed otherwise.'

'You look fine to me, but go ahead. We've got plenty of time before the first appointment.' Evan smiled at her and, for the first time that day, her spirits lifted.

'I promise I won't take long.' She pulled her house key from her bag and led the way to her front door.

'I thought we could get some lunch on our way to the first house.' Evan stepped into the hall behind her.

'Fine.' She was very aware of his proximity and moved away quickly down the hall, talking as she walked, to cover her nerves. 'How many appointments have you made?' Nathalie hung her scarf on the coat hook and carried on through into the kitchen.

'I've three booked. Two look promising. The third one is a bit of a long shot. I didn't find it through the agency, actually Jerome recommended it.' Evan leaned on the kitchen doorframe and watched her as she opened the fridge.

'Would you like a drink while you're waiting?' Her hand shook as she reached for the juice carton and she hoped he couldn't see it.

'I'm fine, thanks.'

'Are they all near town?' She spilled droplets of orange on the counter top as she poured some juice into a glass. Her nerves felt shot to pieces after her appointment and being so close to Evan in a small space.

'Fairly near. I had to think about Polly's school.'

Nathalie was aware of his dark blue gaze levelled on her as she took a welcome drink of the cooling juice. All of her senses were on red alert. 'Great, I'll nip upstairs and get changed. I won't be long.'

'I'll wait right here.' He stepped back from the doorway to allow her through.

She scooted past, giving him a wide berth as she went by. Nathalie thought she saw the hint of smile on his lips as she headed for the stairs.

Once safe inside her room, she took another long draught from her glass and turned to her wardrobe. She caught a glimpse of her reflection in the mirrored door and was surprised to see two feverish-looking spots of colour high on her cheekbones.

'This is ridiculous!' Nathalie pulled a pair of jeans and a warm sweater from the cupboard and changed in a hurry. Before she returned downstairs she took a moment to refresh her makeup and tidy her hair, relieved to see her colour had settled back to a more normal tone.

As she re-entered the kitchen Evan turned round from his position by the window.

'I was admiring your garden and watching your cat.' He nodded his head toward the window. Nathalie followed his gaze and saw Min stalking a long-dead leaf across the emerald surface of the small lawn.

'Min, the scourge of leaves everywhere.' Nathalie smiled.

'Polly wants a pet. She'd like a pony, but because of her asthma, I've been a bit wary of letting her get too close to animals.' Evan looked thoughtful.

'What does her consultant say?'

'He's left it up to me. Polly doesn't have an allergy to animals, at least not one that we're

99

aware of. I'm just a bit overprotective, I suppose.'

'I can understand that.' Nathalie watched Min pounce on her prey.

'Well, we'd better leave if we're going to get lunch before the first appointment. I've got the agents' details in the car for you to see.'

Evan watched Nathalie discreetly from his position at the counter while he waited to place their food order. The café was busy, considering it was the middle of the week, and as soon as a table had become free, he had insisted Nathalie sit down.

Her pallor concerned him and he felt certain that when she'd arrived at her home earlier, she'd been crying. He hoped everything was alright for her. She'd mentioned an appointment, and from her reddened eyes, he could only guess it hadn't been good news.

He ordered two coffees and their food from the harassed-looking waitress behind the counter, then walked back to take his seat opposite Nathalie.

'You look cold.' Without thinking, he reached across the table and took one of Nathalie's hands in his. He felt, rather than saw, the faint tremor in her fingers.

'I'll warm up when the food gets here.'

'Your hand is freezing.'

She made no attempt to disengage herself from his grip. 'You know what they say, cold hands and warm heart.' Yet her smile didn't reach her eyes.

Nathalie had always hidden her true feelings behind a wall of wisecracks and smart remarks. Although, as he thought a little more about it, Evan realised that wasn't strictly true. At one time, she had been prepared to share her feelings and her heart with him. Six years ago, before he'd blown his opportunity.

'What do you think of the properties?' He inclined his head towards the details spread out on the table in front of them.

'They look nice. Though, that one looks as if it might need a lot of work. I take it you haven't anything on the place Jerome has recommended?' She lowered her eyes and studied the paperwork in front of her. He suspected she felt reluctant to meet his gaze.

The waitress arrived with their food and Nathalie slipped her hand from his as they hurried to clear a place on the table for the plates and drinks.

'Enjoy your meals.' The waitress hurried away.

'This looks nice.' Nathalie picked up her cutlery and surveyed her meal of salad and fish.

'It's a little different from the Langstone country club?' Evan suggested. He knew from Jerome that Nathalie could usually be found at all the smart places, so he'd been nervous about bringing her to a small tearoom on the edge of town.

'You know me, if the company is good then I'm happy anywhere,' she joked.

'Do I take it you're paying me a compliment?'

He watched a rosy blush creep over her cheeks as she realised what she'd said. 'Maybe.' Her tone sounded noncommittal as she began to eat her fish.

'That's a shame.'

She glanced at him as her cheeks bloomed pinker then looked back down at her plate again. 'Which property do you prefer?'

She'd steered the conversation back onto neutral territory. Maybe that wasn't a bad thing. Being with Nathalie stirred all the feelings he'd had for her before. He longed to recapture those emotions, but she had been so cool towards him he doubted it was possible.

'The stone-built house with the land looks as if it might be a possibility. It's a shame there's no photograph with that one. I might be able to grant Polly her wish of pony ownership.' He followed Nathalie' s lead for the time being. Maybe if they could start to chat like they'd always used to, he might be able to break through the wall she'd built around her heart.

He longed to know where she'd been earlier, what had happened to make her cry. He had to regain the trust between them, but how? If he asked too many questions like he had the other day she would just close off from him.

'Evan, could you pass me the tartare sauce please?' She looked puzzled and he realised she must have asked him the same question more than once.

'Sorry.' He passed the sauce boat across and watched her spoon a generous dollop of sauce onto her plate.

'You were miles away.' She put the spoon back in the sauce boat.

'Sorry.' He placed his cutlery on his plate and picked up his coffee. 'I seem to be apologising a lot lately.'

The wary expression was back in her eyes

and her shoulders were rigid. 'You're the man who knows the law. Isn't there something people plead when they don't feel like answering someone's questions?'

'I'd say sorry again, but I don't think I'm ever going to be able to apologise enough to you, Tali.' For a split second he saw the hurt he had caused her once again resurface on her face and his heart ached with regret.

She placed her knife and fork on her plate with care before dabbing the corners of her lips with a napkin. 'I think we've covered that ground already. We need to move on.' The gentle tone of her reproach stung more than if she had shouted.

He pushed his plate away with meal unfinished. His appetite had gone.

Nathalie forced herself to continue with her meal. She didn't enjoy rebuking Evan. His apologies had sounded sincere and she had no doubt that he truly wanted her to forgive him.

In many ways, she wanted to erase the events of the last six years and go back to how they had been before, but it just felt impossible. Too much water had passed under the bridge. He hadn't trusted her then with the truth, could she trust him now?

She glanced at her watch. 'Do you think we should leave?'

Evan frowned and pulled back his cuff of his jacket to check the time. 'I guess you're right. Have you finished your meal?'

'Yes, thank you.' She picked up her bag and Evan stood up to assist her with her coat. Her pulse quickened as she shrugged into her jacket, conscious of his body close to hers. She could smell the faint musky scent of his cologne and she swallowed hard. Evan left some notes on the table to cover the bill and tip, while Nathalie walked outside to his car.

He opened the door for her and held out his hand to help her in. Nathalie's skin tingled as his fingers closed over hers for the second time that day. It had taken all her concentration not to betray her feelings when he had held her hand at the table.

She moved her hand from his as soon as she thought it polite, murmuring her thanks as she slid onto her seat. Her heartbeat pounded in her ears and her palms felt sticky with sweat.

Evan programmed the satellite navigation system for directions to the first property on the list and Nathalie busied herself with re-reading the house details yet again.

The journey to the first house on Evan's list didn't take as long as she'd expected. The property stood at the end of a short country lane not far from the main road that led from town. They sat for a moment in the car, looking at the outside of the building.

'What do you think?' Evan asked.

'It looks newer than it does in the photo on the details.' She cast around for something positive to say.

The house was built of garish red bricks while the window frames were of dark wood. Two large conifer trees stood quite close to the building and on a murky winter afternoon the house looked dark and depressing.

'You don't like it, do you?' Evan looked at her.

Nathalie shook her head. 'I can't say it's a house that appeals to me, but it might be nice inside,' she suggested.

'I must admit I'm not keen on the exterior. Still, the owners are expecting us so we'd better go and take a look.'

Half an hour later they returned to the car and Evan put the property details inside the glove-box. 'I think we can rule that one out.'

He turned the car around and programmed the sat-nav with the details for the next property on the list.

'I don't think they'd been strictly honest with their descriptions on the details,' Nathalie mused.

Evan burst out laughing and after a second's pause Nathalie joined in.

'You're telling me! I think we both need a lesson in estate-agent-speak.'

'Mmm, who would have guessed 'classically decorated' meant they had an Egyptian-themed bathroom complete with scarabs and a mural of the Sphinx?' Nathalie wiped tears of laughter from the corners of her eyes with the back of her hand.

'I think I liked the Greek columns in the dining room the best.'

'Just the columns or the nude statues, too?' Nathalie teased. Any remaining tension between them disappeared and she realised she enjoyed having fun with Evan like this – like they had done in the past.

He shook his head, a wide grin on his face. 'I can't wait to check out the next one. How is it described in the details?'

Nathalie smoothed the brochure out on her lap. 'It says, "Old world charm, original features, scope for improvement." I can't wait.' She read him the other key points.

A moment later Evan pulled up at the kerb outside the second property.

'Well?' he asked.

Nathalie looked at the rambling stone house in front of them. The slate roof sagged in the middle and the paintwork had peeled away from the window frames. The path was overgrown with weeds and a wooden gate leant drunkenly on one hinge against the garden wall.

'It's got old world charm, remember?' She tried to keep the laughter out of her voice.

'It's definitely got original features,' Evan agreed.

'The owners have seen us. Come on.' She grinned at him and they got out of the car and walked up the path together.

Twenty minutes later they returned and Nathalie placed the property details in the glove-box, with those of the first appointment.

'Well, there was room for improvement.' Evan started the engine and waved to the elderly owners who stood at the front door.

'Oh yes, I'd say adding an indoor toilet and maybe one or two other modern conveniences would improve it considerably.' Nathalie laughed.

'It did have plenty of charm, but what a money pit! It would make a great project, but Polly and I need somewhere that's ready now.' Evan frowned and reprogrammed the sat-nav for the third time. 'Let's hope this last place that Jerome's suggested will be better.'

Nathalie settled back and Evan turned on the radio, tuning in to a local station playing hits from a few years ago.

'What has Jerome told you about the house?' Nathalie asked.

'It's empty and I've got the keys. It belongs to a friend of his who recently inherited it. The owner doesn't want to live there himself as he lives in Scotland, so he plans to put it on the market. He hasn't placed it with an agent yet as it's only been vacant for a short time.'

'It sounds interesting,' Nathalie observed. Perhaps Jerome had done something useful for once. Her older brother wasn't best known for taking responsibility.

The road they were following led them further out of town than the other two houses, but soon they turned off down a small lane before turning again down a long driveway between two rows of trees.

The driveway ended in front of a house built of faded blue-red bricks. A portico supported on stout stone columns covered the top of the front door to protect visitors from the elements, and on either side of the house lay fenced pasture land.

'Oh, Evan.' Nathalie turned to him. 'Is this it? It's beautiful.' Even in the gathering twilight, the building looked elegant and homey. A family house waiting for a family to live in it once more.

Evan stopped the car on the gravel turning circle in front of the house. 'I guess I don't need to ask you what you think of this one.' He smiled at her and pulled a set of keys from his jacket pocket.

He climbed out of the car and came around to open her door. They stood still for a moment in the dusk, looking at the exterior.

'It's like a doll house with the sash windows.' For a split second Nathalie forgot the house was just for Evan and Polly. She could see herself in that house, with lights in the windows and smoke coming from the chimney, Polly playing by the hearth, Evan working in his study, and the smell of fresh bread in the kitchen.

'Let's see if the interior matches up to the exterior.' Evan slipped his arm through hers and together they crunched their way over the gravel to the front door.

Chapter Seven

Evan searched through a large bunch of keys ready to unlock the front door of the house. Once the door was open Nathalie tried to shake off the strange feeling of homecoming that washed over her as she stepped over the threshold into the hall.

'There's a light switch over here.' Evan flicked it to fill the hall with soft yellow light from a beautiful Venetian glass chandelier. The crystals sparkled in the light from the candle bulbs which made them flash and twinkle in a waterfall of light.

'Wow!'

'Double wow! As Polly would say,' Evan agreed.

The hall floorboards looked dusty, as did the staircase which was of carved oak with barley twists on the balustrades.

'You are sure Jerome gave you the right address?' Nathalie touched the newel post with a tentative finger and left a trail in the dust.

'The key fit.' Evan smiled at her.

She followed him through a panelled door leading off the hall into a large sitting room. The cornices were deeply moulded plaster while wooden shutters hung at the windows. The fireplace was white marble.

'It's too good to be true. There has to be a problem.' Nathalie span around, laughing.

Evan laughed with her. 'Maybe we'd better see the rest of the house, to be on the safe side.'

They explored the remainder of the empty house together, opening the doors to admire the generous sizes of the empty rooms.

'It needs a new kitchen and some of the tiles in the main bathroom need to be replaced.' Nathalie led the way back down the staircase.

'But compared to the last place, this house needs hardly anything done.' Evan paused on the stairs to look around.

'You're right there. The last place needed to be demolished. Are you going to make an offer?' She stopped on the bottom step and turned to look at him.

'What do you think? This house is great, a real family home. It's a place to grow into. Polly will love it.'

Nathalie turned and walked into the hall. She didn't even know why she'd been getting excited. The house was for Evan and Polly, for a family. Evan's family. There were enough bedrooms to expand if he had more children.

'Are you okay?' Evan stood behind her and placed his hand on her waist.

'I'm fine. It's gone a little cold in here.' She rubbed her hands on the tops of her arms, stepping out of Evan's reach. She did her best to ignore the little stab of pain in her heart.

He checked his watch. 'You're right. It's getting late, and we should head back.' He opened the front door for Nathalie before switching off the light and securing the house.

'It looks as if my big brother has finally done something good by finding you this place.' Nathalie forced a smile.

'I'm glad you came with me.'

'I've enjoyed it.' She was sincere. She had enjoyed being with Evan and looking at the properties. She squashed the sad, sorry-for-herself feeling back down into her stomach.

'I'm grateful. It's so much better having someone else with me. Two people notice things that someone on their own doesn't.'

'I think you'd better make sure you call the owners as soon as possible. A house as nice as this won't stay on the market for long.'

Evan pulled his phone from his jacket pocket. 'No time like the present.'

Nathalie gave him a thumbs-up sign before strolling a little way off so he could talk in privacy.

She walked over the gravel driveway to the side of the house and leaned on the wooden fence to admire the view across the field. There were buildings at the bottom of the paddock. It looked as if there might even be a ready made stable for Polly's pony.

'They've accepted the offer.' Evan's voice, next to her, startled her out of her reverie. Lost in her own thoughts, she hadn't heard him approach.

'That's fantastic! I assume everything will move quite quickly as the house is empty and you haven't a property to sell?' She straightened up from where she had been resting her arms on the top rail of the fence and thrust her hands into her pockets.

'I hope so. The sooner Polly is settled, the better. Mum has been very good letting us stay with her, but Polly needs her own room with her own things. She's been very insecure since the divorce was settled.'

'Have you heard from Laurel?' Nathalie wished she hadn't asked. It wasn't any of her business if Evan kept in touch with his ex-wife. Any questions she asked would make him think she was being nosy, or worse – jealous.

'I expect she'll be in touch when she wants something.' Evan sounded resigned, rather than bitter.

'You know you'll have to let Polly have her pony now you're buying a house with all this land.' Nathalie gestured toward the field. She wanted to get off the subject of Laurel.

'I expect you're right. Come on. I'll run you home. You look half frozen.'

Nathalie took a step towards the car and felt her boot slide on a patch of loose gravel. Evan moved swiftly, to cup her elbow as she wobbled off balance.

'Hey, better be careful.'

Nathalie steadied herself against him. Her pulse raced as Evan continued to hold her arm as they made their way to the car. 'Did you hurt yourself?'

'No, you caught me before I fell on my bum.' Nathalie tried to make a joke, and hoped Evan wouldn't notice the heat which had flared in her cheeks.

'It's a very cute bum.'

She flushed even more.

'Tali, I know we said we'd just be friends,

but I can't help the way I feel when I'm around you.' His eyes were serious as he studied her face.

'Don't do this to me. You've only been back here two minutes and you're turning my life upside down.' She pulled her arm away from his hand. Her body trembled with emotion.

'I've spent the last six years wishing I'd done things differently, hoping at some point I could make things up with you and maybe get a second chance.'

Nathalie turned away, and tried to blink back the tears in her eyes.

'Tell me honestly, Evan, what do you want for your future?'

He spun her back around to face him, 'We had something very special together, Nathalie. We wanted the same things in life.'

'That was then. Darn it all, I've had enough of today.' She wrenched open the door of the car and climbed inside.

Evan stalked around to the other door and got into the driver's seat. 'I wish you'd tell me what's wrong. It's more than just what happened between us in the past. I know you too well, Tali. You were upset when I called to pick you up today.'

Nathalie pulled a tissue from her coat

pocket and dabbed at her eyes. 'Please, just take me home. I don't want to discuss it. I can't.'

He started the engine and flicked a quick glance at her. Nathalie kept her eyes fixed straight ahead, determined not to look at him.

'Are you going to tell me?'

Nathalie ignored him. Her private life was none of his business. What if she did tell him about her problems? He would either tell her the doctors could be wrong or start suggesting folk cures, just like anyone else she had ever entrusted her secret to.

Worse still, he might look at her with a pitying expression in his eyes and treat her like some fragile piece of china to be protected from the harsher things in life. At least this way she kept her pride. It saved her the hurt of being rejected because she could never have children if she were the one to reject him first.

Evan's mobile phone rang on the tray of the dashboard.

'Can you get that for me? It might be the vendors calling back.'

Nathalie hesitated for a second, before she picked it up. At first she couldn't quite take in what the agitated woman on the end of the line had said.

Then the words made sense. 'Evan, it's the school calling about Polly. She's at the hospital.'

He checked the traffic behind him and swung off the road on to a grass verge. Nathalie handed him the phone, her heart thumped with fear for his little girl.

He listened intently, his face paled as he spoke. 'Okay. Thank you, we're on our way. Tell Polly I'll be there as fast as I can.'

He disconnected the call and threw the phone onto Nathalie's lap. 'Polly's in the paediatric emergency room at the hospital. She had an asthma attack at the after school club.' His jaw was taut with pain as he pulled back out into the traffic and gunned the engine.

'Is she all right?' Nathalie forgot her own worries.

'That was the woman who runs the club. She called an ambulance when Polly didn't respond to her inhalers and she's with her at the hospital now. So are the doctors. Damn this traffic!' He thumped the steering wheel with frustration as they got caught up in the early evening rush-hour traffic of the city centre.

'It's a good hospital. The paediatricians

have a great reputation. We'll be there in a minute. Here, take this next left turn. I know a short cut.' Nathalie directed him through a maze of narrow back streets behind the hospital until they reached the car park.

Evan pulled into the first available space.

'I know the way to the emergency rooms. I've been here often enough.' Nathalie linked her arm through Evan's in a gesture of reassurance, resting her hand firmly on his forearm. He placed his other hand on top of hers as if taking strength from her presence.

'I just hope she's okay. I shouldn't have sent her to school today. She's still got a nasty cough.'

'If you kept her home every time she had a cough she would never go out. You can't blame yourself. Dad always says asthma is very unpredictable, especially in children. Come on, let's go and find her.' Nathalie longed to hold him close to her and reassure him.

He allowed her to steer him through the different departments. His rapid pace was almost a run in his hurry to reach his child, until they reached the paediatric emergency reception desk.

Evan stepped up to the counter. 'I'm

looking for my daughter, Polly Davies.'

The woman behind the desk checked her monitor. 'She's in cubicle three, Mr Davies. Doctor Chen is with her at the moment. If you could just sign this form for me then you can go through.'

Nathalie hung back a little from the desk. She longed to know if Polly was alright, but felt as if she were intruding somewhere she had no right to be by accompanying Evan any further.

Evan, however, finished signing the hospital paperwork then looked round for her. 'Come on.'

She accompanied him through the swing doors and down the corridor until they came to a curtained-off area.

Polly looked so small and frail on the big metal trolley bed. A green oxygen mask covered her face and a drip was attached to her arm. The male doctor listening to her chest straightened up as Evan and Nathalie entered the room. A young woman with an anxious expression rose from her seat in the corner.

'Oh, Mr Davies, I'm so glad you're here. I'm Mrs James from the four o'clock club. I came with Polly in the ambulance,' she said as she stepped forward.

'How is she?' Evan's gaze was fixed on Polly.

Polly's big blue eyes opened at the sound of her father's voice, but she was clearly too exhausted from the asthma attack to attempt to talk.

'She is okay now, we've stabilised her and given her some steroids. The I.V. is a precaution for shock and the oxygen will help her lungs to recover.' The doctor rushed to reassure him.

'She looks much better since we got here,' the school supervisor added.

Evan stooped to kiss Polly's blonde hair. 'I got here as fast as I could. Thank God you're all right.' He stroked her pale face with a gentle finger.

Nathalie's eyes filled with tears of relief for both of them. The journey to the hospital had brought back unhappy memories of when Nate, her twin brother, had been involved in a bad car accident a few years earlier.

'If I might have a quick word with you, Mr Davies?' The doctor opened the curtain and indicated to Evan to step outside.

The school supervisor moved to leave. 'I have to go home, if you don't mind. Normally I'd stay, but it's my son's cub night and I'm already late.' The woman smiled an apology at Nathalie and Evan, squeezed Polly's hand in farewell and slipped out of the cubicle.

'I'll stay here with her.' Nathalie took Polly's other hand in hers. Evan looked at her for reassurance, and then stepped out into the corridor in order to talk to the doctor.

'Hi Polly. You gave us all a bit of a fright, there.' Nathalie smoothed the little girl's tangled curls, her heart filled with tenderness for the sick child who still struggled to breathe. Polly managed a feeble half smile in reply from under her mask.

Her school bag had been placed next to the chair where the after-school supervisor had sat. Nathalie could see a small piece of familiar-looking worn, pink fabric poking out of the top. She released Polly's hand for a moment and opened the bag.

'Look who I've found in here.' She lifted Polly's favourite doll out from among the school books and placed it in the little girl's arms. Polly hugged the battered toy close to her.

'You're being so brave. I hope I'll be brave like you when I have to stay in hospital for my operation to make me better.' Nathalie smiled at her.

Polly relaxed back against her pillows and Nathalie pulled them into position so she was still upright.

'When you're back at home and feeling better I'll come and see you, then you can show me those dolls of yours.'

Evan stepped back through the curtains into the cubicle. In his hands he carried two Styrofoam cups of tea. 'I thought you might like a drink.' He handed Nathalie one of the cups. 'Thanks for staying with Polly. I gave Mrs James the money for a taxi home. It seemed the least I could do.'

'Thanks for the tea.' She accepted the drink gratefully. Her throat felt dry with stress and from the long afternoon of property hunting.

'I see Pookie went to school with you again.' Evan touched his daughter's face with a tender finger and smiled at her.

'She looks a little better,' Nathalie ventured. Polly's lips seemed to be regaining some of their normal pink colour and the unnatural pallor had begun to lift from her face.

'The doctor wants you to stay here overnight, Poll. I've phoned Nanny and she's going to bring us a bag. The doctor says I can stay with you,' Evan explained.

A tear slid down the side of Polly's face.

Nathalie wiped the tear from the child's cheek with the edge of a clean tissue from her pocket. 'It's just for tonight, darling. The sooner you get better the sooner I'll come to your house to see you. I'll bring you a present of something very special and Princessy from my shop, I promise.'

Polly lifted her hand to hold Nathalie's.

'That'll be something to look forward to.' There were strain lines around Evan's eyes, but his expression was warm with gratitude.

A nurse bustled into the cubicle, clipboard in hand. 'Miss Polly Davies? I'd better check you over before the porter comes to move you up to the children's ward.' She wheeled over a blood pressure machine and began to attach a Velcro cuff to Polly's arm.

'I should go.' Nathalie put down her half-drunk cup of tea on top of the locker and edged towards the curtain. Suddenly, she felt awkward and in the way.

'Polly and I are really glad you came.' Evan glanced at his daughter.

'If I go over to the Post-grad now, I can get a lift home from Daddy. It's his teaching afternoon with the medical students.' She hitched her bag further onto her shoulder. 'Will you call me and let me know how she is?'

'Of course.' He took both her hands in his. 'Thanks again, Tali. For everything.'

His lips brushed her forehead and a shiver of delight ran through her body from her head right down to her feet. She opened her eyes and pulled her hands free. 'Bye Polly, I'll see you soon.'

Polly gave Nathalie a weak wave with her fingers as the nurse undid the cuff from her arm.

Then, seizing her chance, Nathalie slipped out of the cubicle and walked swiftly away along the corridor towards the exit.

'Hello Daddy. Any chance of a lift home?' Nathalie popped her head around the half-open door of the office.

'Nathalie! What a pleasant surprise. I was just about to leave.' Her father looked up from the pile of case notes on his desk. 'Are you coming back for supper? You know, your mother wants to find out how your appointment went.'

Nathalie grimaced. 'Supper would be lovely.'

'I take it from the look on your face that you're going to go ahead with the surgery.' He lifted off his glasses and placed them in his spectacle case.

'I've a provisional date for the autumn.'

Her father stood up and gathered her in his arms as if she were no bigger than Polly. 'I'm sorry, my dear, but I can't say I'm surprised. I think you're doing the right thing.'

Nathalie closed her eyes and hugged her father, revelling in the feeling of security. 'Thanks, Daddy. A hysterectomy is a big step, but no matter how I look at things, it seems that having my womb removed is the only sensible solution.'

Chapter Eight

'How did your appointment go at the hospital?' Gemma had a cup of tea waiting for Nathalie when she arrived at the shop the next morning.

'I'll need some time off in the autumn. I'm having my surgery then.' Nathalie shrugged.

'I'm sorry.' Gemma's face looked sympathetic. 'At least you won't be in so much pain, though, and you spend a fortune on tampons. Hey, think of the money you'll save!' She joked in what was clearly an attempt to lift Nathalie' s spirits.

Nathalie smiled at her friend. 'Trust you to turn a negative into a positive.' She took a sip of tea.

'More to the point, how did you get on with Mr. Hunky yesterday?' Gemma leaned across the counter, her eyes alight with curiosity.

'You are so nosey! He's put an offer in for a house.'

Gemma raised an eyebrow. 'So, he'll be looking for a housekeeper then?' she hinted.

'Gemma! Actually, he's got other things on his mind at the moment. His little girl was taken ill yesterday afternoon while we were out. He's spent the night at the hospital with her.'

'Oh, that's awful! Is she all right?'

'I rang the ward this morning before I left home and they might let her go home later. She has asthma and I think this sort of thing has happened before.' Nathalie cradled her mug in her hands.

'You're very fond of that little girl, aren't you?' Gemma mused.

'Yes, I am. She's a lovely child.'

'Her dad's not so bad, either,' Gemma remarked and winked at Nathalie.

'You are hopeless! Stop trying to play matchmaker.'

'That's rich, coming from you. How many times did you try to set Nate up with someone before he fell in love with Jenni?'

Nathalie grinned. 'Okay, you might have a point,' she conceded.

'Have you told Evan about your illness?' Gemma asked after a few minutes' pause.

Nathalie drank the last of her tea and moved across to the sink to wash her mug. 'No.'

She heard Gemma cross the small room to

stand beside her, then felt a comforting arm across her shoulders, hugging her. 'Don't you think you should?' Her friend's voice sounded gentle.

Nathalie thought about it. Perhaps she should tell Evan about her problem. It wasn't fair to prejudge his reactions and he seemed worried about her. 'Maybe, I don't know.'

'It's not the end of the world, not being able to have children. If he loves you, and I for one think he does, he'll understand.' Gemma tightened the hug for a moment.

'I'll think about it,' Nathalie replied, and moved away to place her mug back in the cupboard.

She left Gemma on the shop floor while she cocooned herself away in her office. She opened her ledger ready to start the paperwork, but her thoughts kept wandering away from invoices and payments and back on to Polly and Evan.

When she'd rung the children's ward at breakfast time, she'd expected to speak to a nurse, but instead they had put Evan himself on the line to talk to her.

He had sounded weary as he'd answered her questions about Polly, having spent the night lying on a camp bed at her bedside. Nathalie guessed he hadn't had much sleep.

She sighed and tapped the end of her pen thoughtfully against her cheek. Gemma had made a good point earlier. She ought to tell Evan about her illness. A secret had come between them once before – only then it had been Evan who hadn't placed his trust in her. Wasn't she guilty of the same thing by not telling him her secret?

The phone rang and startled her out of her reverie. 'Hello, Bridal Belles?' She answered without thinking.

'Hi Nathalie, its Evan.' The sound of his voice coming so fast behind her thoughts about him made desire pool in her stomach like liquid amber.

'Is everything okay?'

'Fine, I was just ringing to let you know Polly and I are home.'

'You must be exhausted.' She could picture his face, blue eyes shadowed with tiredness and his jaw dark with stubble.

'I'll be okay once I've grabbed a shower and had something to eat. Polly's lying on the sofa watching television.' His voice rumbled low and husky in her ear.

'It sounds as if she's on the mend.' Nathalie wondered if Polly missed her mother at times like these. Her heart ached for the little girl. From what Evan had told her about Laurel's relationship with Polly, Nathalie doubted if the model would cancel her engagements or drop everything to be with her sick child.

'Children heal quickly. That's one good thing I've learnt from Polly's problems,' he said.

Nathalie felt the smile in his voice. 'I promised Polly I'd visit her once she was home. Would it be okay if I call in tomorrow?'

'Of course. She'd love to see you.'

'Tomorrow it is, then. I'll come once I've closed the shop.' She replaced the phone in the cradle, glad that Polly seemed better.

The phone rang again straight after Evan had finished talking to Nathalie.

'Hi, Evan.' The fake mid-transatlantic twang of his ex-wife's voice resonated from the receiver.

'Hello, Laurel.' He peeped through the hall door into the lounge where Polly was still engrossed in the television before pulling the door shut. 'What can we do for you?' He hadn't bothered attempting to track Laurel down to tell her about Polly's hospital admission. He knew from past experience that she wouldn't be interested.

'Can't a mother just call to check on her

baby?' Laurel's voice took on the pouty, little-girl tone she always adopted when she wanted something.

Evan's heart sank. The last thing Polly needed now that she had begun to settle in her new surroundings was her mother upsetting her all over again.

'Most mothers, yes. But let's be honest, Laurel, you're not the maternal type.'

'Maybe, but she's still my daughter,' Laurel snapped, all pretence at pleasantry at an end.

'What do you want?' Evan felt too tired to hold an argument with Laurel, especially when there was a risk that Polly might overhear.

'I'm flying in tomorrow and I want to see Polly.'

'She's not very well at the moment.'

Laurel didn't wait for him to finish. 'Bring her down to London. I'm staying at the flat.'

'She's not well enough to travel; she spent last night in hospital. You'll have to come here if you want to see her.' He wondered what else was on Laurel's agenda. She usually only asked to see Polly when she wanted something.

'Oh, that's very inconvenient!' Laurel huffed.

Evan gritted his teeth. 'You're welcome to come here to see her.'

'Are there any good hotels?'

'There's a five star country club, The Langstone. I'll book you a room.'

'Make sure it's a suite. I can only spare one night, I've something exciting to tell Polly.'

Evan suppressed a sigh. Whatever Laurel had to tell Polly probably wouldn't be good. It never was. 'Do you want me to tell her you're coming?'

'Of course. I'll be there Saturday morning.'

'We'll look forward to it.' The irony in his voice went over Laurel's head and she rang off.

He opened the door to the lounge and went through to break the news to Polly of her mother's visit.

'What does she want?' Polly's reaction was much the same as his own had been. Laurel had hurt her daughter too often in the past for there to be much trust between them now. Even so, hope was mixed with the wary expression on Polly's small face.

'She wants to see you. She said something about some exciting news she had to tell you.' Evan hugged his daughter, cuddling her up close on the sofa where they both sat.

Polly sighed and picked at the stitching of the fleecy throw which covered her legs. 'She doesn't want me to live with her again, does she, Daddy?'

'I don't think so. This is our home now. I'll take you to see our new house soon when you're feeling better.' Evan did his best to reassure her.

'I don't want to live with Mummy.' A tear rolled down Polly's face and Evan's heart squeezed in pain.

'Hey, no tears. You're staying with me – it's all settled, remember?'

Polly sniffed and snuggled up against him.

'I phoned Nathalie earlier. She's coming to see you tomorrow.'

Polly's face brightened and she sat up. 'Is she bringing me a present?'

Evan laughed. 'I don't know, you'll have to wait and see.'

Polly settled down with a contented expression to play her doll.

It didn't take very much to make Polly happy, Evan decided as he held his daughter close. But he wished Laurel would try a bit harder to put Polly first in her list of priorities. Sadly, he could never see that happening. The only person on Laurel's list was Laurel herself.

A bigger contrast in personality to Nathalie would be hard to find. When he'd first met Laurel he'd been taken in by her good looks and apparent charm. They'd only dated for a few weeks before he'd realised that her charm only existed if there was something for her to gain from it.

His brief relationship with Laurel had been the biggest mistake of his life, excluding the fact that it had given him Polly. He'd thought when they had broken up and he'd returned to his hometown that he'd never see her again.

Then, when he'd become reacquainted with Nathalie and they'd begun to date, he'd fallen in love for the first time in his life. Their lives had been in front of them. They'd made plans and discussed the future. He'd intended to ask her to marry him.

Then, out of the blue, Laurel had dropped the bombshell of her pregnancy and everything had changed. One meeting with her had convinced him that she wasn't going to be a fit person to care for a baby alone – not least his baby – and so he'd proposed.

He kissed the top of Polly's head. For a lawyer, he'd been pretty stupid, but how could he regret Polly?

Nathalie waited on the doorstep for Evan to answer the bell. In her hand she had a small gold gift bag which contained Polly's present.

'Hello, Nathalie.'

Evan still looked tired. He must have been at work, because he still wore his dark grey business suit.

'I'm not disturbing you, am I?'

'No, come in, Polly's waiting for you.' He led the way into his mother's sitting room. Polly sat on the floor in her pyjamas, a row of dolls lined up next to her.

'What a lot of dolls!' Nathalie smiled at Polly.

The little girl's face lit up when she saw the bag in Nathalie's hand. 'I got them all ready to see you. I told you I'd got lots of Princess clothes for them.'

'I've got something special for you, too.' Nathalie beckoned her to come and sit by her on the sofa. Evan sat opposite them in one of the armchairs and slackened his tie as he watched.

Nathalie passed the bag to Polly. Her heart pounded as she watched Polly open it. She hadn't been too sure what a small girl like Polly would really like, but she'd wanted it to be something special.

'Oh!' Polly gasped her mouth a small 'o' of astonishment as she drew out a tiny gold crown made of filigree threads.

'I thought every princess should have their own crown. So, this one is yours.' Nathalie took it from the child's trembling fingers and settled it on top of Polly's blonde curls.

'Daddy, look! I'm a princess!' Polly turned to Evan, her eyes shone with excitement.

'Princess Polly.' He smiled at her then his eyes locked with Nathalie's and she read the silent thank-you that was expressed there.

'Can I go and show Nanny?' Polly bounced to her feet.

'I think you should say thank you to Nathalie first,' Evan reminded her.

Polly threw her arms around Nathalie and hugged her tightly. 'Thank you.' Then she let go and went skipping from the room.

Nathalie was conscious of silence growing in the room. 'She looks much better. The antibiotics must be working well.' She plunged into speech, determined to fill the gap.

Evan rubbed his face. 'I'm hoping she'll be able to go back to school on Monday.' Lines of exhaustion pulled at the corners of his eyes.

Nathalie longed to cross the room and kiss

his strain away. She pulled herself up at the craziness of her thoughts.

'I appreciate you coming to see Polly. The asthma attack has unsettled her again, just as she was about to get to know her new classmates.' Evan pulled his tie from round his neck and undid the top button on his shirt.

His simple action caused the breath to catch in Nathalie's throat. She realised how hollow her protestations to Gemma about Evan being just a friend had been.

'You look exhausted.' Her eyes lingered on the open neck of his shirt. Darn, she had to stop staring.

'I didn't get any sleep at the hospital and Polly is awake a lot in the night. Her medicine makes her hyper and when she lies down, the coughing starts.'

'Are you working from home?'

'For the moment. I'll probably go to the office tomorrow. Mum's going to stay with Polly.' He folded his tie and placed it across the arm of the chair. 'Let me go and make you a drink. Tea or coffee?'

Nathalie felt awful that he planned to wait on her when he looked as if he'd like nothing better than to go to sleep. 'I don't want to be in the way.'

'Polly will be back in a minute. Mum's gone to have a lie down,' Evan assured her.

'I'll have coffee then, please. Can I do anything to help?'

Polly came twirling back into the room. She'd dressed herself in a ballerina skirt over the top of her pyjamas. The gold crown was still perched on top of her head and she waved a toy wand in her hand.

'You look lovely.' Nathalie smiled at the comical sight. Evan raised an eyebrow and shook his head in disbelief at his daughter's outfit. 'I'll get you a drink, Tali.'

Polly picked up all her dolls and started to show them all to Nathalie. By the time Evan returned with a tray of cups, the sofa was covered with toys. Nathalie was unused to playing with small children and had felt awkward at first when Polly had instigated a game.

Much to her surprise, though, when Evan handed her a mug of coffee she realised she had enjoyed herself. She had avoided contact with children for a long time, ever since she'd realised it was unlikely that she would have any of her own.

She'd been pleased when friends had become pregnant – of course she had – but it had hurt too. It had been easy to hide her pain by buying generous gifts for the new arrivals. But then she had lost touch with many of her friends as their children had grown up, only sending gifts for birthdays and Christmas.

'It's hard to tell who's enjoying that game the most,' Evan remarked as his daughter started to arrange the dolls in a circle ready for a tea party.

Nathalie smiled at him as he cleared a space on the far end of the sofa and sat down. 'I never played with dolls when I was little. With my brothers around there was always something else to play with that looked more fun, like racing cars and bows and arrows.'

Polly gave her a pitying look. 'Poor Tali, you can share my doll.'

Evan grinned and Nathalie couldn't help smiling back at Polly's generous offer.

'Don't you have a doll of your own at all?' Polly asked.

'No. Grown ups often don't,' Nathalie explained.

'Well, when you're poorly and have to go the hospital for your operation I'll come and visit you. You can borrow one of my dolls then to help you get better.' Polly concentrated on placing plastic tea cups in front of her dolls.

Evan shot her a questioning look and Nathalie felt the colour begin to rise in her cheeks. She'd forgotten that she'd told Polly about her planned surgery.

'Operation? I didn't know you were ill. It's nothing serious, I hope.' Evan leaned forward, his face concerned.

Nathalie could feel the faint heat from his body and smelt the hint of musk from his cologne as he moved nearer. 'It's not till the autumn. Women's problem.' She tore her gaze away from his and busied herself with drinking her coffee.

She knew he suspected there was more to know. She would have to tell him the truth, but not while Polly was in the room. 'I really should go now. I bet it's almost your bedtime,' she said to Polly.

Polly looked disappointed. 'Will you come again?'

'Maybe. Perhaps your Daddy will bring you to the shop and you can look at the pretty dresses.' Nathalie suggested as she reached for her handbag.

'Can we, Daddy?' Polly begged.

'I suppose so, as Tali's invited you. Tidy these toys away and I'll be back in a minute.'

Polly gave Nathalie a farewell hug, and then Evan escorted Nathalie to the front door leaving Polly in the lounge.

'Thanks again.' Evan leaned on the door frame.

'I've enjoyed it. She's a beautiful little girl.' Nathalie's pulse roared in her ears. She knew he would ask her about Polly's remark.

'Is it a big operation?' His eyes were fixed on her face and she knew he'd worded his question with care.

'Pretty big. It – It'll mean I can't have children.'

There, she'd said it. The words were out. Evan continued to stare at her, a stunned expression on his face.

Chapter Nine

Silence stretched between them.

Evan straightened up from his position on the doorframe. 'Tali, are you okay? I mean is it serious?' He looked bewildered.

'I'm fine. It's a condition I've had since I was a teenager. As I've got older, it's got worse and I'm at the point now where a hysterectomy is my best option.' She scanned his face for his reaction. She couldn't remember ever feeling as scared as she did now, as she waited for his response.

He came down the step towards her, the lines of his face harsh in the moonlight. 'There's no tablets that you can take? Nothing else they can offer you?' He placed his hands on her arms and gripped her gently as if to prevent her escape.

'No. I've had all the tablets and minor surgery before. This is it now. There isn't anything else.' It felt weird to voice out loud all the things she had been hearing in her head ever since the appointment.

'So, now you know. That's where I was on

Wednesday morning, why I was late getting home.' She tried to school her voice so the true extent of her anguish wouldn't show.

'How long have you known about this?'

'Like I said, it started when I was in my teens, but back then everyone was optimistic. You know, try this drug or that one. Then they always dangled the carrot of a pregnancy maybe clearing things up and making me better.' Her voice trembled.

'Won't that work now?' Evan's voice sounded hopeful and Nathalie wanted to scream with frustration and hurt. Did he think he could be the answer to her problems?

'The problem with this condition is that although sometimes pregnancy can cure it, it's virtually impossible to get pregnant when you suffer from it. It's progressed too far with me now.' She saw realisation dawn in his eyes and knew she'd said enough. 'I have to go. I've a busy day tomorrow.'

He released her and she walked away as fast as she could without giving him the chance to call her back. She reached the sanctuary of her car and drove off without a look back. Tears poured down her cheeks and plopped in hot, salty splodges on the steering wheel.

'Oh, I'm so stupid!' She dashed her hand across her cheeks and pulled in a deep breath of air. What else had she expected from Evan? The rather impassive reaction she'd got had been just what she'd expected. It was all her fault for dropping such a big bombshell on him.

Nathalie pulled to a halt in front of her house. Deep in her heart she'd pictured a different outcome. One where Evan had taken her in his arms and sworn he didn't care that she couldn't have children because he would always love her no matter what.

'Stupid!' she whispered. She'd misjudged the depth of his feelings for her. When he'd talked about a dream of the future, he must have had a different picture in his mind from the one in her heart.

Even so, as she opened her front door, she hoped her phone would be ringing. That he would call her and want to comfort her and be with her. She tossed her keys onto the kitchen counter. The answerphone was silent. Only Min waited patiently next to an empty food bowl

Nathalie opened the cupboard to get some food for her cat. Min wrapped herself around Nathalie's ankles as she replenished the dish.

'Go on, ring me, darn you!' Nathalie muttered and willed Evan to call her.

By the time she'd made and drunk a soothing cup of hot chocolate it was clear she
wasn't about to hear anything. Her heart
ached as she snapped off the lights and
trudged upstairs to bed with Min at her
heels. 'I guess I'm better off knowing he
can't deal with this now, rather than further
on down the line.'

The cat stayed silent.

'You look wrecked. Bad day?' Gemma
asked. It was mid-morning and the rush had
begun to slow down.

'A bad life, more like.' Nathalie scooped up
a bundle of hangers and dropped them into
an empty linen basket behind the counter.

'You told Evan?' Gemma grimaced.

Nathalie pulled a cloth from under the
counter and began to polish the front of a
display cabinet. 'Let's just say it didn't go
well.'

Gemma frowned and crossed the shop
floor to stand next to Nathalie. 'What happened?'

'He asked a few questions. The usual,
can't they cure you? Are you sure? Then he
didn't really say anything else.'

'Oh.'

Nathalie looked up from her polishing at the disappointed note in Gemma's voice. 'Yeah. "Oh" about sums it up. Still, I'm better off now, aren't I? I mean I won't set myself up to get hurt all over again.'

'Are you sure about that?' Gemma asked.

'I'm sure.' Nathalie resumed her polishing, determined not to cry in front of her friend.

Gemma looked out of the window. 'I hate to make a bad day worse, but Karen's coming.'

'It's okay, I'll deal with her.'

The shop bell jangled and Karen breezed in. 'Just thought I'd call and see how everything's going. It's the rehearsal and dinner on Wednesday, don't forget.' She pulled her planner from her bag.

'Everything is in hand. Are the bridesmaids coming tomorrow for their final fitting?' Nathalie tucked her duster out of sight and steered Karen across to the counter.

'Yes. My fitting is right before the rehearsal, isn't it?' Karen peered over Nathalie's shoulder at the shop diary.

'That's right. The seamstress will be here in case there are any last-minute adjustments.' Nathalie snapped her diary shut. She knew Karen had tried to glean information about the other clients by peeking.

The shop bell jangled again and a delivery man came in with an enormous basket of dark red roses.

'Oh, aren't those gorgeous!' Gemma and Karen exclaimed together.

'Delivery for a Miss Nathalie Mayer?' The man read from a clipboard he carried in his other hand.

'Tali, they're for you,' Gemma breathed.

'Wow, you must have an admirer?' Karen's face was alive with curiosity.

Nathalie quickly took the basket from the man. 'Thank you.' She moved away and rested the flowers on the counter. Karen and Gemma crowded around as the delivery man left.

'Open the card,' Gemma urged.

'Who are they from?' Karen asked.

Nathalie's hand trembled as she slid the small white card from the envelope, even though she already knew who they must be from.

'Evan!' Karen announced in a triumphant voice before Nathalie had a chance to hide the card from view.

Nathalie pushed the card into the pocket of her jacket. 'Can you take these through into the back of the shop please, Gemma?'

Gemma looked puzzled. 'I'll put them in your office.'

'Just friends, hmm?' Karen queried.

'The flowers were a thank-you for something I'd given his daughter,' Nathalie fibbed. She didn't want Karen to spread her private life all over town. Unfortunately, she had a feeling it might already be too late. Karen had drawn her own conclusions.

'Are you bringing him to my rehearsal dinner?' Karen asked.

'I told you, no. We aren't on those kinds of terms.' Nathalie felt herself flush.

'Well, those flowers look to me like the kind a man sends to a woman when he wants to be on those sorts of terms.' Karen picked up her handbag ready to leave. 'Dark red roses? Please. Those are the flowers a woman gets the morning after a night well-spent with a man.' She nudged Nathalie's arm. 'And you look as if you didn't get much sleep last night.' She swept off out of the shop.

Nathalie was left to stare after her in outraged silence.

'What did she say?' Gemma emerged from the back of the shop.

'Oh, that woman! She drives me crazy!'

'What did the card say?'

149

Nathalie reached inside her pocket and pulled it out. Evan had written it himself. She recognised his penmanship and the distinctive fountain pen he always used.

'We need to talk – Evan,' Nathalie read the message aloud.

'You should call him,' Gemma advised.

The shop bell jangled again and a woman accompanied by two excited little girls came in. Gemma went over to meet them. Nathalie stared at the card for a moment longer then returned it to her pocket. More customers soon entered the shop, which meant she had no choice but to put off her call till later.

All too soon, it was time to close. Throughout the afternoon Nathalie had tried to work out what she would say to Evan when she did call him.

'Do you want me to stay while you lock up?' Gemma offered.

'No, its okay, you go.'

Nathalie saw Gemma out and locked the door behind her. She fingered the card in her pocket as she walked into her office. The smell of the roses met her in the doorway, rich and dark. The petals were soft and velvety under her touch as she stroked the largest flower. It reminded her of Jenni's wedding bouquet and the ridiculous superstition. Then, before she could change her mind, Nathalie picked up the phone and dialled Evan's number.

'Voicemail.' She replaced the receiver on the handset without leaving a message. She still didn't have any clear idea of what she wanted to say beyond thanking him for the bouquet.

Evan had switched off his mobile the minute he judged Laurel's plane to have landed. He felt thankful he wouldn't need it for work over the weekend. Laurel would give him no peace if it was left on.

He wondered if Nathalie had liked her flowers. All day long he'd been kicking himself for his failure to react properly to the bombshell she'd dropped about her illness. Her news had taken him by surprise and by the time he'd recovered his wits, Nathalie had gone.

Polly knelt on a chair at the kitchen table with her colouring pencils.

'That's a nice picture.' He admired her handiwork. The picture was of a man and a woman holding hands with crowns on their heads. A drawing of a little girl with yellow hair, also wearing a crown, was next to them.

151

'That's you and Nathalie getting married,' Polly explained. 'I'm in my princess dress because I'm the bridesmaid.'

Evan swallowed. 'Um – Poll, sweetheart, Nathalie and I are just friends. We aren't getting married.' Even as he said the words out loud, he knew he wanted to marry Nathalie, had always wanted to many Nathalie. The revelation quickened his pulse as it hit home like a thunderbolt.

'I saw you kiss her. I peeped round the door when she said goodnight. That means you'll marry her,' Polly declared confidently as she began to colour in Nathalie's hair in the picture with a black fibre-tip pen.

'Poll, it's not that simple, okay?'

His daughter silenced him with a look and a shrug of her shoulders. At least he should be grateful that Polly didn't want him to remarry Laurel.

He toyed with the idea of calling Nathalie but he felt the initiative needed to come from her. If he pushed too hard at the moment, he could make everything worse. He rubbed his hand through his hair in frustration. The cases he dealt with in court weren't as tricky to handle as Nathalie and his feelings for her.

The house phone rang and he rushed to

answer it, hoping it would be her.

'Your cell phone is off. I've been calling ever since I arrived.'

'Hello, Laurel. Where are you?' His heart sank as his ex-wife's peevish tones hit his ear.

'I'm at this crummy country club. Thank God I'm only here for one night. Bring Polly over after breakfast,' she commanded.

'What time?' He knew Laurel seldom started her day early when she wasn't working. Breakfast could mean any time up to twelve noon.

'About ten. Is she there now? Put her on.'

Evan gritted his teeth. 'Polly, Mummy's on the phone.'

Polly heaved a dramatic sigh and walked across the kitchen to take the receiver from him.

'Hello.' She listened for a while with a bored expression on her face. 'We can go into town. Okay, see you tomorrow,' She hung up without handing the phone back to her father.

'Mummy's going to take us into town for shopping tomorrow.' Polly announced and went back to her drawing.

'That's nice.' Evan tried to put a positive spin on things. Polly liked to shop and an outing in the fresh air might do her some good. The forecast for tomorrow was mild, so it shouldn't trigger her coughing. The big downside was that they would be spending the day with Laurel.

Nathalie slept badly. All evening she had turned over in her mind what she planned to say to Evan, yet again without any success. She had picked the phone up several times to call him but had lost her nerve each time. Consequently, by the time she'd gone to bed her nerves felt as if they had gone through a cheese grater.

Min seemed to sense her mistress's discomfort and Nathalie was late leaving for the shop. Her appointment book was full, several brides and bridesmaids were due in to try on dresses. The seamstress and her Saturday staff were already inside the shop with Gemma by the time Nathalie arrived.

'You don't look as if you caught up on your sleep,' Gemma observed in a low voice as she shepherded Karen's bridesmaids towards the fitting rooms.

Nathalie sighed. Her make-up techniques must be slipping. The perfume from the roses Evan had sent filled the shop. It had been raining when she'd left the previous night, so she'd decided to leave the flowers at the shop. She'd moved them into the fitting area to make the place look nice. Already several customers had admired and commented on them.

She would have to phone Evan tonight, or maybe call and see him. It wasn't like her to be a coward or to put unpleasant things off but this was an exception.

It was almost lunchtime before she managed to escape into the back to make a mug of tea for herself and Gemma. The last of the morning's customers for the seamstress were in the fitting area and Gemma had just taken a deposit on a very expensive, one-of-a-kind wedding dress.

The shop bell jangled as she lifted the teabags from the mugs. As everyone else was occupied, it looked as her cup of tea would have to wait. Nathalie groaned, dropped the teabag into the bin, and went back onto the shop floor.

'Nathalie!' A familiar blonde-haired little girl ran forward and hugged her around the waist.

Nathalie looked up from Polly's excited face to see Evan accompanied by a woman whose face she'd seen on a hundred magazine covers. She was fair-haired like Polly and dressed more for a night on the tiles instead of an English market town's high street on a Saturday afternoon.

'I brought Mummy to see your shop,' Polly explained.

Laurel extended an immaculately manicured hand. 'My daughter insisted we come. I hope you don't mind.'

Nathalie shook Laurel's cool fingers and noted that the smile on Evan's ex's mouth didn't reach her eyes.

'I told Laurel and Polly that Saturday wasn't a good day to visit.' Evan's arms were folded and his stance defensive.

'Oh, but this is such a sweet little shop,' Laurel cooed.

'Thank you,' Nathalie said, as Polly slipped her small hand into hers. There was an uneasy atmosphere and she had the feeling that this was no chance encounter.

'I met a friend of yours and Evan's yesterday when I arrived at the hotel. She told me so much about you.' Laurel flicked her gaze up and down Nathalie's figure. 'Then when Polly suggested calling in, well, it would have been rude not to come and meet you. My daughter has been singing your praises all morning.'

A shiver ran up Nathalie's back. She

hadn't imagined the ice in Laurel's voice. It almost sounded as if the model was jealous.

'You'll have to forgive me, but I can't imagine who you could have met.'

Laurel's scarlet lips curved into a smile. 'A woman called Carol, or Karen, or something like that. She was at the hotel as I checked in. She told me about the lovely roses Evan sent you. Very romantic.'

Nathalie sucked in a breath. Evan's expression had darkened at Laurel's words.

'You must mean Karen Gillespie. She's a client of mine.' Nathalie tried to keep her voice even, although her legs shook as she wondered what else Karen could have said.

'Come on, Polly. I think we should be going now that we've said hello to Nathalie. She really is very busy.' There was the hint of impatience in Evan's voice as he held out his hand to his daughter. His face looked like thunder and Nathalie guessed that calling in to the shop had not been his idea.

'It was nice to meet you,' Nathalie said to Laurel. From the looks the model had given her, Nathalie was in no doubt that Laurel had called in specifically to warn Nathalie off Evan. Why, though, she couldn't imagine. Unless Laurel and Evan planned to get back together. That couldn't be possible, could it?

Not after everything Evan had said about his relationship with his ex?

'The pleasure was all mine, believe me,' Laurel purred as she followed Evan and Polly out of the shop.

Chapter Ten

'Wow!' Gemma came across the shop and gave Nathalie a hug. 'Are you okay? I thought you were going to pass out.'

'I'm fine. I'd like to get my hands on Karen's scrawny neck, though.' Nathalie took a deep breath to try and calm her agitated pulse.

'I wouldn't like to be in Laurel's shoes if Evan gets hold of her out of his daughter's sight,' Gemma observed.

'It's Polly I feel sorry for.' Nathalie could see why Evan had applied for custody. She wouldn't trust Laurel any further than she could throw her based on what she'd just heard.

'Yeah, poor kid! What a witch!' Gemma shook her head as she walked away to return to her customers.

Nathalie retired to the back room and took a long draught of her almost-cold tea. Normally, Laurel would have caught the rough edge of her tongue, but, Polly's presence had made Nathalie keep her speech in check.

She finished her tea, wrinkling her nose in displeasure at the cold dregs. Gemma's mug still stood on the counter full of cold tea so Nathalie poured it away and put the kettle back on. Her resolve hardened as she waited for the water to boil. Tonight, she would phone Evan and find out once and for all where she stood with him. She made Gemma a fresh drink then went back onto the shop floor to relieve her.

It was late when Nathalie arrived home. A last minute flurry of customers had kept all of them busy long after their usual closing time. She pulled her coat off in the hall. The answer phone was silent, the light still green. No messages.

Nathalie kicked off her shoes and wandered through to the kitchen. Min trotted across the tiled floor at the sound of the fridge door opening.

'I'm looking for something for my dinner, not yours,' Nathalie rebuked her cat as she studied the contents of the shelves. She pulled out a block of cheese and some butter. 'Looks like cheese on toast tonight, Min.'

She fixed herself some supper and sat down with her tray in front of the television. She'd just taken her first bite when the phone rang.

'Nathalie, we need to talk.'

She swallowed her mouthful of cheese as fast as she could. Her pulse pounded. 'Evan, I was going to call you. Thank you for the flowers.' She ground to a halt, still unsure of how to word what she wanted to say.'

'Laurel insisted on calling in on you today. Polly had been singing your praises and I think Laurel was curious about you. She came to tell us she's moving permanently to California.' He spoke in a measured tone that she assumed he normally kept for the courtroom.

Nathalie sighed. 'About the other night–'

'I wanted to talk to you about that, you took me by surprise.' His voice sounded low and husky in her ear.

'Evan, you don't have to explain anything.'

'I've been worried about you. I knew something was wrong when you pulled up outside your house the day we went to look at properties together. I didn't know what it was; if you had financial problems, family problems, or something else. I didn't like it.'

Nathalie nibbled on her lower lip in her anxiety, as he paused. 'Evan, I think maybe this has all been a mistake.' She raced the words out in a hurry.

'I don't follow you.' He sounded bemused.

'I meant you and I, renewing our friendship.' She hesitated. 'Relationship' hadn't been the right word, yet 'friendship' wasn't it, either. To her dismay her voice thickened and she choked on her words as she continued. 'I can't have children, Evan. I can never give you the family you want, or brothers and sisters for Polly.'

'I see.'

'I think we should stop seeing each other, at least for a while.' She delved in her pocket for a tissue.

'Does this decision have anything to do with Laurel's visit?' he demanded.

She dried her eyes quickly. 'No. Although, Polly seems to be getting quite attached to me.'

'And that's a problem?' She heard ice in his tone.

'No. I mean, yes. Maybe.' What did she mean? She wasn't sure what worried her most. Polly becoming too attached to her, or Nathalie losing her heart to the little girl who'd held her hand so trustingly this afternoon.

'What are you trying to tell me, Tali?'

She wished she could see his face, explain what she meant. 'I can't do this anymore.' How could she explain how it had felt to have his daughter look at her with so much trust on her small face? What it did to her when Polly held her hand?

The line went dead. She listened to the disconnected buzzing sound and replaced the handset. He'd hung up on her. The pain in her chest hurt as much as if she had received a physical wound.

She sat for a moment and waited to see if the phone would ring again before she pushed her plate aside. Her appetite had gone, replaced by a cold, sick feeling in the pit of her stomach. What had she done?

Nathalie dashed the tears from her face then carried her plate of half-eaten toast to the kitchen. The metal lid of the bin clattered as, moving like an automaton, she threw her scraps away.

It was over. Gone. Her dream of a life with Evan and Polly disposed of as tidily as the crusts from her plate. She wandered upstairs and swapped her tailored work suit for comfy cotton pyjamas. The elastic waistband felt soothing across her tense abdomen.

Once changed, she gathered up her fleece blanket and headed back downstairs. One more trip to the kitchen to gather her supplies of white wine and chocolate and she installed herself on the sofa to watch a DVD of her favourite film.

'My own private pity-fest.' She scooped Min up to sit beside her as she snuggled up under her fleece. She had lowered the blinds against the sleet that drummed in the darkness against the windows and switched on her lamps. Nathalie tried to lose herself in the film, which had always been a tried and trusted remedy for past heartbreak. This time it appeared to have lost some of its magic.

The sound of her doorbell intruded, and Min jumped down and stretched, ready to trot into the hall. Nathalie peeped through the slats of the wooden blind at her front window. The water splashes on the glass blurred her view but her pulse quickened as she made out the soaked figure on her front step.

Evan spotted the movement of the blind and his eyes met hers. She froze for a second and her pulse pounded in her ears. In the light from the porch she noticed his hair had been darkened by the sleet and plastered to his head as he waited for her to open the door.

Nathalie dropped the blind and hurried into the hall. She didn't know what to say, what to expect. Her fingers shook as she

164

slipped the security chain free to open the door.

The light from the hall spilled out to where Evan stood on the front step. Nathalie was suddenly conscious of how she must look.

'Do you think I might come in?' He made a slight gesture with his open hands at the sleet that pounded the ground around him like silver bullets.

She stood aside and he stepped into the hall. Water ran from his jacket in rivulets onto the laminate floor.

'I had to come and see you.' A white layer of melting slush lay along the lines of his shoulders.

'You're wet. Let me take your coat.' The sound of the water dripping galvanized her into action and she took the wet jacket from him. 'Go through and dry off by the fire.'

She wiped the sweat and melted sleet from her palms against the legs of her pyjamas as she fetched him a towel.

'Thank you.' His fingers brushed hers as he took it and heat scorched her skin at the brief contact.

'I didn't expect to see you again. You hung up.' Nathalie held her breath as she waited for his reply.

'I didn't hang up. I was on my way here

and lost the reception.' His hand stilled in the act of rubbing his neck and face dry. 'Was that really what you thought? That I'd hung up on you?' His hair had spiked into damp tufts where he had towelled the sleet away.

She let out a breath. 'I didn't know what to think. You didn't call back.'

Evan dropped the damp towel onto her coffee table. 'You should have known I wouldn't let you go a second time without a fight.' The lines of his face seemed intensified by his feelings.

'Evan, I told you on the phone, I can't–' She gasped as he took a step toward her.

'What can't you do?'

'Evan, I can't have children.'

'And have I ever asked you to?' He grasped her arms and compelled her to look him in the eyes. 'Tali, just tell me the truth. Do you love me? My feelings for you have never altered. I love you. I want us to be together: you, me and Polly.'

Nathalie swallowed hard. 'I've always loved you. Polly is a wonderful little girl.' She hesitated. His hands gripped her, warm but firm, refusing to release her until he had his answer.

'But?' She saw hurt cloud his eyes.

'What if you want a brother or sister for Polly later on? You might regret being married to a woman who can't give you a son or who can't give your daughter a brother or sister.' Regret might eat into their relationship like acid, stripping it away until there was nothing left.

'I love you, Nathalie. No one gets married because of a guarantee that their partner is fertile! Our family will be complete with the three of us.'

'You don't know that you won't change your mind.' She longed to believe him but she had seen and heard too many stories where the happy-ever-after part had failed to materialize. She'd given her heart to him before and believed it was safe.

'Sit down. There's something I need to tell you.' He steered her across to the sofa where he sat down beside her. His shoulders hunched as he leaned forward. 'When Laurel told me she was pregnant, I had doubts about whether Polly was really mine.'

Nathalie gasped in surprise. 'But she looks just like you. She has your eyes!' Evan's love for Polly was so secure she couldn't believe he'd ever had doubts about her paternity.

'I realized quite quickly that Laurel wasn't going to be ideal mother material. When

Polly was born and I saw her lying in that plastic crib so tiny and helpless...' He shook his head. 'All the thoughts I'd had about getting a DNA test vanished. I held her in my arms and she opened those big blue eyes.'

Nathalie folded her arms across her chest to protect herself from the shaft of pain in her heart. Why was he telling her this? She would never know the magic of holding her baby in her arms. 'What happened?'

'I didn't pursue a test. As time passed and Polly got ill, she needed me. She looks like me. Any doubts I had faded. Then when I set the wheels in motion to divorce Laurel and gain custody of Polly she announced that Polly wasn't my daughter after all.'

Nathalie's hand flew to her mouth. 'That's terrible!' How could anyone be so cruel?

Evan's hand balled into a fist. 'I felt as if my world imploded. I didn't know what would happen to Polly, how this might affect her, or even if it were true. I was angry at myself.' His jaw clenched and Nathalie knew it was a struggle for him to keep his emotions in check.

'You got Polly, though?'

'I insisted on a test. The result didn't really matter in some ways because Polly was mine in my heart, no matter what. I just didn't want Laurel to have a hold over us. Fortunately the results were conclusive.'

'I can't imagine what you and Polly have gone through.' Nathalie ached at the thought of all Evan and his daughter had suffered.

'I love you, Tali. I'm never going to change my mind, no matter what the future might hold for us. When I thought I might lose Polly I felt so empty, so incomplete. Without you in our lives I'd have that same feeling.' He took her hands in his, the warmth of his fingers on hers somehow spreading to warm her very soul.

His lips brushed against hers and her mouth parted in response, tasting the sweetness of all he had just offered her. She surrendered to the tenderness of his kiss as desire built within her.

'So, you haven't given me an answer,' he murmured against her lips.

Nathalie broke away from his kiss, her pulse thudding in her ears. 'I love you, Evan. You and Polly. I guess in some ways I've used my problems as a kind of shield. It's been a reason not to get close to anyone or for them to get close to me. Yet, I always wanted someone to be my hero. Does that make me sound pathetic?'

He caressed the side of her face with his hand. 'You never needed anyone to be your hero, Tali. You've coped with your illness all this time, knowing your dream of a baby of your own wasn't going to be possible. I'd say you were your own hero.' He kissed her tenderly on her forehead.

Nathalie raised her head to see the love he had for her shining in his eyes. 'I love you.'

He kissed her again, making her skin tingle with his touch. Nathalie snuggled closer, revelling in the scent of his skin and the rhythmic beat of his heart. Safe and secure in his arms with no more secrets between them, she knew she'd found her hero after all.

Two months later, Nathalie took her place next to Evan on the front row of chairs in the school hall.

'I hope she's okay.' Evan whispered as he took her hand in his, the emerald of her engagement ring glinting under the light.

'She'll be fine. She's had some of her inhaler and she looks beautiful,' Nathalie reassured him.

'She's rehearsed this so many times.' Evan shuffled on the hard wooden chair.

'Shush, it's starting.'

The lights dimmed and a small girl in a

flowing pink dress and gold crown stepped onto the stage. Polly beamed at the audience and recited the lines she'd practised. Nathalie mouthed them with her, tears of pride in her eyes as she watched her daughter perform in the Easter production.

In less than a month's time Polly would have another starring role, as a bridesmaid at Nathalie and Evan's wedding.

The publishers hope that this book has given you enjoyable reading. Large Print Books are especially designed to be as easy to see and hold as possible. If you wish a complete list of our books please ask at your local library or write directly to:

Magna Large Print Books
Magna House, Long Preston,
Skipton, North Yorkshire.
BD23 4ND

This Large Print Book, for people
who cannot read normal print,
is published under the auspices of

THE ULVERSCROFT FOUNDATION

... we hope you have enjoyed this book.
Please think for a moment about those
who have worse eyesight than you ...
and are unable to even read or enjoy
Large Print without great difficulty.

You can help them by sending a
donation, large or small, to:

**The Ulverscroft Foundation,
1, The Green, Bradgate Road,
Anstey, Leicestershire, LE7 7FU,
England.**
or request a copy of our brochure for
more details.

The Foundation will use all donations
to assist those people who are visually
impaired and need special attention
with medical research, diagnosis
and treatment.

Thank you very much for your help.